"Not that the story need be long, but it
will take a long while to make it short."
— Henry David Thoreau

Living on Water

Matt Cohen was born in Kingston, Ontario and educated
at the University of Toronto. He is the author of several
novels, including the critically acclaimed quartet, the
"Salem novels", and most recently, *Nadine*. His work has
been translated into several languages.

Well known for his short stories, including *Columbus
and the Fat Lady* and *The Expatriate*, this is his first
collection since *Café Le Dog*.

Matt Cohen and his family live in Toronto.

LIVING
ON WATER

Matt Cohen

Penguin Books

PENGUIN BOOKS
Published by the Penguin Group
Penguin Books Canada Ltd, 2801 John Street, Markham, Ontario, Canada
L3R 1B4
Penguin Books Ltd, 27 Wrights Lane, London W8 5TZ, England
Viking Penguin Inc., 40 West 23rd Street, New York, New York 10010, USA
Penguin Books Australia Ltd, Ringwood, Victoria, Australia
Penguin Books (NZ) Ltd, 182-190 Wairau Road, Auckland 10, New Zealand

Penguin Books Ltd, Registered Offices: Harmondsworth, Middlesex,
England

First published in Viking by Penguin Books Canada Limited, 1988
First published in Great Britain, 1989
Published in Penguin Books, 1989

10 9 8 7 6 5 4 3 2 1

Manufactured in Canada

Canadian Cataloguing in Publication Data
  Cohen, Matt, 1942-
    Living on water

  (Penguin short fiction)
  ISBN 0-14-010915-3

  I. Title.

  PS8555.038L58 1989   C813'.54   C88-094136-7
  PR9199.3.C64L58 1989   72499

British Library Cataloguing in Publication Data Available

"The Zeidman Effect" and "Remember Me to London" were originally
commissioned by *Anthology* for broadcast on CBC radio. They were first
published in *The Canadian Forum* and *Canadian Author and Bookman*.

With thanks to DL and RW

LIVING ON WATER

Contents

Lives of the Mind Slaves

Lives of
the Mind Slaves

When sandstorms, freezing cold, or sudden bursts of rain caused Nellie to cough or hesitate, Norman would caress the steering-wheel and murmur encouragingly, "Come on, Nellie. You can make it, Nellie." Or in desperate circumstances, "Nelliebelle honey, I love you." Nellie was a 1962 Ford V8. In her youth she had been maroon, a dark lustrous red endowed with flowing curves and a motor that could snap your neck back when you pressed her pedal to the floor. Those had been Nellie's salad days, the days and nights of her first youth, the years of careful washes and hand-shining, valve-jobs and cylinder re-fittings, the days when her engine always hummed with clear creamy oil and when her evenings were spent at drive-in movies, her springs gently rocking.

Nellie's first owner had cried real tears when he sold her to Norman. The deal took place in downtown Vancouver, outside a liquor store. That was where Norman saw her first. Drawn by her glowing curvaceous body he stepped closer to look at the FOR SALE sign taped inside a window. He was still wondering whether to copy down the telephone number when a man appeared beside him, kicking the tires, stroking the fins, talking in a low steady mumble which ended, "You wouldn't believe the loving I had in this car. But now the wife wants a station-wagon for the kids." The lover was a wispy-haired pot-bellied man with a sad smile.

Norman was tanned and streaky blond from a summer planting trees on Vancouver Island. The year before he had been crowned by a Ph.D. — an accomplishment rewarded by a job teaching reme-dial English to immigrants in Halifax. This was followed by his months on the island. There Nor-man met his first Nellie: a young woman who wore white running-shoes and wanted to make love to him every night all night. Then arrived a letter from the McGill-Queen's University press offering Norman a contract to turn his thesis on "The Roots of Symbolism in American Narrative" into a book. Norman was lying on a beach as he opened the envelope. Reading the letter he felt the sun burn brighter. So it was good-bye to Nellie the human and hello to his new driveable Nellie. Destination: three thousand miles across the continent to McGill, where he had earned his degree, for six months of post-doctoral research. He didn't finish the book, but another piece of luck came along — the offer of an actual appointment, one-year ex-tendable, at the University of Calgary. A proud event, his first full year teaching, but due to a sudden plunge in the departmental budget the appointment was not renewed. Fortunately the sympathetic department chairman helped him find a life-saving two-year term as a sessional lecturer at the University of Winnipeg — at a much lower salary than he had been receiving in Calgary. After Winnipeg it was back once more to McGill for another two-year appointment, this time on the understanding that he would finally finish his book and — if he did — take his place in the pantheon of the tenured.

Between cities, jobs, universities, was the desert. The desert was emptiness. The desert was life with no future. Also, like any desert, it was dry and thirsty. Although during the day the sun burned hot, the night was cold and scary. Likewise fine weather was followed by storms of obfuscation. Life would have been not life at all had the dry and stormy desert not been punctuated by oases in the form of congenial pubs where fellow mind slaves could always be found. And after the slaking of thirst — so many thousands of mugs of draft had been consumed that Norman had the permanent taste of foam at the corners of his mouth — followed manna. Manna was love. Manna was emotional relief. Manna was the security of flesh compared with the insecurity of jobs with no future, students with no talent, tenured professors with no compassion. Manna was the pressing of body to body, the rites of sex the point of which was not so much ecstasy — though ecstasy he would not have refused — but the complicity of imperfect nakedness and sex, the sequel of long talks in the darkness about whether life in the desert could ever give way to something better.

At McGill the first time, he had met Elisabeth.

Dark, slim, with a brittle pretty face and a sharp laugh, she was a Blake specialist who taught part-time and most evenings spent an hour in the pub sipping beer before going home to make dinner for her lawyer husband. Norman was twenty-six then, Elisabeth almost thirty.

The second year in Winnipeg, she showed up again. By this time Norman was himself pushing thirty; and that year he developed the uncomfortable habit of looking closely at himself as he shaved. Lines had started to grow out of the corners of his eyes, his mouth had begun to take a particular downward turn, his hair which had been dramatic during the tree-planting summer was now brown, except at the temples where dustings of grey had mysteriously settled. Worse, the nights at the oases followed by manna/mamma had begun to sour. The love of many gave way to the love of one. When a fourth-year student dazzled and pursued him, he fell in love. After that it was no longer mind over matter, but vice versa. Love and jealousy, storms of passion and lightning moments of pure happiness. Then she had gotten pregnant. The pregnancy was announced in the summer after graduation. The girl, whose name was Ruth, told Norman about it one day at breakfast. As she leaned over the coffee, blue eyes opened wide and trusting — or so Norman believed at the moment — Norman had a picture of himself with a beautiful blue-eyed daughter in the circle of his arms. "Let's get married," he said.

That afternoon Ruth broke the news to her parents, who were big givers to the alumni fund. Scenes ensued. The parents, who had envisioned a brilliant academic future for their precocious daughter, complained to their good friend the university president. Ruth decided on an abortion. Norman was informed that although — technically — he had broken no laws and therefore could not be sued, his appointment would be terminated at the end of the following year. By September Ruth, womb scraped virgin clean, was off to graduate school at Harvard while Norman was left to contemplate his disgrace and his future.

When Elisabeth walked into the pub Norman didn't recognize her right away. Her face was fuller, and demarcation lines of bitterness divided eyes and cheeks. As it turned out, she no longer had a husband, but there was a child. It was two years old and like a queen talked about herself in the third person: "Mona wants a cookie. Mona wants ice cream."

"Mona wants to talk. Mona wants to sit down. Mona wants television." Norman took up with Mona. Every Saturday afternoon he called for her; once or twice a week he collected her at the day-care centre, then brought her home and fed her dinner. He told Elisabeth about what had happened to him with Ruth; she told Norman about her marriage. Recounting past disasters, struggling through a difficult evening with Mona, looking at Elisabeth across the kitchen, Norman felt as though he and Elisabeth had constructed for themselves a sort of shelter for battered survivors, an emotional refuge in which they were the patients, slowly healing, and Mona, unbeknownst to herself, the physician. One night Norman — to help himself get through a particularly excruciating set of essays — brought over a bottle of scotch and his six favourite Miles Davis records. Near midnight he became aware that he was upstairs, in the bathroom, splashing water onto his face. He raised his eyes to the mirror; his cheeks looked yellow and numb, which was also how they felt. When he stepped into the hall something in his blood went to sleep. "Something in my blood has gone to sleep," he said. Elisabeth was downstairs, listening to Miles Davis. She had her own essays to worry about and, Norman realized, they made her far too busy to be concerned about dormant aspects of his blood. He turned. He looked into Elisabeth's bedroom. She had a large bed and it was empty. Soon he was lying on his back. Time passed. Then he was lying on his belly, on top of Elisabeth. The light from the hall made her eyes glow, and the face that had been growing so familiar now seemed to belong to a stranger.

At the beginning of November Ruth phoned. Just her voice was enough to set him seething, whether with love or despair he had no idea. "I'm dying without you," she said. Norman, sitting alone in his half-furnished apartment, looked at his cold wooden floor littered with unread books, indigestible essays, the remains of half-eaten meals. "I'm dying without you," she had said. Norman wondering what it was he was doing without her. "Well?" she asked. Any protective layer he might have formed was now shattered. "Will you come to see me?"

"Yes," Norman said, his voice choking. And then Ruth said some things about how she had missed him and what she was eager to do to him when he arrived.

"This will be my most embarrassing moment," Norman announced to Elisabeth, thinking even as he spoke how odd it was that people like Elisabeth and him, chattels to a system which despised them, were in fact so enslaved that a clever little phrase could grease the stickiest situation. But Elisabeth agreed to take his classes so that Norman could have a long weekend in the Promised Land.

The bus left Winnipeg at dawn. By the time the stony grey light of morning had filled the sky, they were on the highway. Thirty-six hours later he arrived in Boston — palms sweating, clothes soaked in cigarette smoke, stomach knotted from tension and white-bread sandwiches. Ruth, all smiles, received the weary traveller in her scented arms, brought him back to her apartment for a night of passionate love. Just as his stomach began to unwind, the recriminations began. Before Norman could unpack the clothes he had so carefully folded, he was on his way back to the bus station.

The last year at McGill, everything went wrong. First, Norman turned thirty-two. Until then he had been able to believe that the sojourn in the desert was a necessary part of the larger story. And, too, he had discovered no lack of fellow wanderers. Fellow, yes; there was strange fellowship in this life after fellowships, fellowship in the expertise in subjects about which no one else would ever care, fellowship most of all in the curious roles they all played —knights errant of the mind, intellectual mercenaries with knowledge for sale at cut-rate prices.

But the week after his thirty-second birthday Norman discovered he had contracted a "social disease." The doctor assured him that it was harmless, relatively speaking, and that a bottle of pills plus a month of abstinence would make him a new man. But they couldn't. Norman had been going seriously with a girl for the first time since Ruth. When confronted with the medical evidence, she admitted she was about to decamp and move in with someone else. "The thing is," Norman wrote to Elisabeth, "this would have been funny a few years ago. The wronged lover comes home to discover that his girlfriend wants to play house with the musician who has just given her VD. But now I'm too old. I don't want my life to be a comedy any more. I want to settle down, be loved, have children, enjoy the fruits of my labours. Is this not the natural destiny of man?"

"No," Elisabeth wrote back, "it is not the natural destiny of man — not of man, mankind, men, or you. If nature has anything in mind for you, Norman Wadkins, it is that, like all matter in the universe, you shall be subject to the second law of thermodynamics, to wit: decline, decrepitude, death."

"Thanks a lot," returned Norman.

"You missed my whole meaning," Elisabeth protested. She wrote her letters to Norman on departmental stationery. Nor were her letters posted from Winnipeg, as they had been in previous years. Now they emanated from Vancouver and were complete with weather descriptions. "Brilliant light. Mountains rising out of mist. Another heart-rending sunset." Even when it rained, Elisabeth persisted in lauding the softness of the falling water. "City of mountains, city of dreams," she called it in one letter. Not just for the scenery, Norman supposed, but also because Elisabeth had arrived at middle age in style: she was in Vancouver as an Associate Professor as well as being Assistant Dean of Women.

"What I mean is that although destiny has nothing special in mind for you, you could do something for yourself. Awake O Blind and Passive One! Join the club of positive thinkers! Have you ever considered being Saved? How wonderful it would be to know that God Was On Your Side. Failing that, you could at least finish that book. Others would kill for a contract with a good university press — you're sitting on yours like a neurotic student afraid to hand in that really big paper. What are you waiting for, Physician? — heal thyself."

When spring came he was offered a one-year terminal extension of his sessional appointment. In other words, they would hire him as slave labour for a final year, if he would promise to go away when it was over. Norman telephoned Elisabeth.

"Is that what you want?"

"Of course not."

"What are you going to do?"

"Tell them to hire me properly or stuff it."

"Good."

The next three days Norman spent writing a letter outlining his experience and pointing out that he was doing, for half the price, the work of tenured professors whose qualifications did not exceed his own. Proclaiming his own virtues, Norman found, was a strange experience. At the pub he complained that it made him feel like a prostitute. In fact, writing about himself he discovered that, parallel to his dubious life of intermittent affairs and jobs grasped in desperation, he had enjoyed a scintillating career grooming illiterates across the giant breadth of the country. By the time he had signed his letter and put it in the mail he was convinced that the university would reward his years of diligence with dignity and affluence.

He was wrong. The day he received his letter of refusal from the university he sold his furniture, his stereo, most of his books, and traded the proceeds, along with a clunker grandmother Nellie that only started in dry weather, for a Nellie young enough to know the meaning of kilometres. This newish Nellie, Nellie LaBelle he named her because he bought her from a woman in the French department, was a Japanese sedan with a leather-wrapped steering wheel, a built-in cassette player, and — Norman discovered when he was already on the highway — a glove compartment full of yearning country-and-western tapes.

From the day he arrived in Vancouver, the sky was always blue. And from Elisabeth's house he could see the mountains, their snow-peaked tops jutting into the sky like jagged postcards.

The idea was that he would live in the basement apartment as a paying tenant. Even so, Norman felt guilty, and insisted that he help Elisabeth by taking Mona to daycare in the morning and picking her up in the afternoon. Then — the idea continued — while the house was empty he would work on the book. But in fact he preferred sitting in Nellie LaBelle and driving around the city. Sometimes he stopped to explore the parks, eat hamburgers if he was hungry or bored, walk along the beaches or through downtown streets. He took on the shopping so he would have an excuse to drive around the city reading notice boards.

Young girl, 18, seeks babysitting. References.

Three men need woman to share two bedroom apartment. Kitsilano.

Moving and other odd jobs. Phone Ray.

Middle-aged couple, will do anything legal.

Norman imagined himself placing his own advertisements:

Male, non-starter, seeks inspiration. Write Norman.

Easterner, reluctant immigrant, wants to be swept away by passionate young woman with private income. Phone Norman.

Notice-board reader, available 24 hours a day, wishes to be kidnapped by illiterate nymphomaniac for serious caring relationship. Find Norman.

The Farradays, Mark and Heloïse, were middle-aged and legal. They did not, however, need to place advertisements. Mark was a one-time physicist who at the age of forty had discarded job, wife and vocation to become a playboy real-estate developer. Ten years later he controlled millions of dollars of half-used space in Vancouver's new downtown office towers, owned an expensive yacht moored in the company of other such yachts, and had re-married to a professor of women's studies with whom he had produced a perfect pair of twins. These five-year-old twins and Mona met at the university day-care centre and insisted on visiting each other. The parents trailed along. "I've explained that you're a friend and not a lover,"

Elisabeth told Norman. "But you don't have to see them if you don't want to."

Curious, Norman went. The Farradays had a cedar mansion on the water; while the children sequestered themselves inside to watch television, the adults sat on the lawn drinking martinis and exclaiming over the perfect weather and the terrific view of the mountains.

"It drives me crazy, too," Heloise said to Norman. "People here talk about the weather as though it were the most important thing in the world. Wait until you've been here a whole year. Summer is always long, winter late, spring early."

By the time dinner came, Norman was on his fifth martini. "I'm a beer drinker," he confided to Heloise in the kitchen. He was also thinking of confiding to her that he found her very attractive, extremely attractive, that in fact he could imagine them melting together. He realized, however, that were he to take his confidences so far, he would have also to add that it was not him speaking, but the martinis.

"Elisabeth tells me you're working on a book."

"Such is the current excuse for my existence," Norman said. Then added: "That was supposed to be clever."

"I know," Heloise said, and then raised her eyebrows as if perhaps she realized all sorts of things deep and misty. In theory Norman's excuse for his existence in the kitchen was that he was helping her prepare the salmon steaks. In fact he was standing by the window, waiting for something to happen.

Then Heloise suddenly smiled at Norman, and Norman found himself looking into the eyes of a woman who did not care he had drunk four more martinis than he should have, a woman disarmed, a woman who could love him for himself alone, a woman offering a whirlpool of possibilities.

"Am I drunk? Am I imagining things?"

"Yes and no," said Heloise.

Norman carried the platter of salmon into the backyard. Mark was standing over the barbecue. He had precise square-fingered hands—hands that were, like the rest of him, perfectly preserved, perfectly in tempo.

Norman placed the steaks on the red-hot grill. "The flesh sizzled," Norman said.

"What?" Mark asked.

"It's the sizzle," Norman said. "Did you ever wonder what it would be like to walk on coals?"

"I did it," Mark replied. "The man around the corner gives lessons. An amazing person, really."

One day after a morning of nothing and lunch at a health-food bar where he felt comfortable reading the paper while he ate, Norman went walking through a park near the beach. In the centre of the park some teenagers were playing basketball. Norman stopped to watch. "You want to play?" one of them called out.

Norman looked down at his feet. He was wearing sneakers. He stubbed out his cigarette. "Sure."

The first time he was passed the ball he dropped it. For a while after that, he just trotted up and down the court, trying to save his breath and remember who was on his team. Then the ball came to him again and suddenly he was running with it, free, his hand bouncing the ball up and down against the packed dirt as though twenty

years had just fallen away. "Go, go!" someone
shouted, and Norman found himself turning to
avoid a check, twisting in towards the basket. Then
he was high up in the air and the ball was sailing
free — sailing past the backboard and into the
grass. An explosion of laughter, a slap on the back.
"Nice try, hey, we thought you might be too stoned
to move!" And then he was running up and down
the court again. As he ran, he was suddenly aware
of the encumbrances of time; the layers of flesh that
formed a girdle around his belly and hips — one
which he wished could now be shrugged off like an
unnecessary heavy sweater. Muscles in his legs, his
back, his shoulders had softened and forgotten
what to do. Dead zones had created themselves in
the nerves that connected mind to body. When he
leapt for rebounds, he found himself tied down by
gravity, his hands batting awkwardly in the air.
Nonetheless the ball began to follow him around.
But instead of trying to shoot he passed it to his
team-mates, slowing at centre court while they
carried on to the other end. By the time half an hour
had passed his lungs felt like wet shopping bags
and the soles of his feet were burning. He crouched,
gasping, at the edge of the court while the others,
shirtless and muscled, played on. Norman looked at
his watch. It was time to pick up Mona. He left
without saying anything and drove to the day-care
centre. When he arrived he was drumming on
Nellie LaBelle's leather-wrapped wheel and singing loudly.

Two days later Norman showed up at the park
again. This time he was wearing anti-blister ban-
dages on his heels and an extra pair of socks. For a

while he stood at the edge of the game—then the same boy who had welcomed him the first time waved him onto the court. The boy was tall and thin with an unlikely cloud of red hair that sprayed out as he leapt, flattened when he ran. Now Norman noticed how easily he moved, how he controlled the traffic around both baskets, how his team-mates passed to him when they were in trouble, looked to him for the ball when they were in the clear. Norman found himself getting the ball more frequently and twice, when he drove for the basket, he actually managed to hit the rim.

"It's coming back," the red-haired boy said encouragingly. As though he, eighteen, fluid as mercury, knew what it was to be blocky and awkward, what fifteen years of drinking beer and smoking two packs a day could do to your body.

"Stick" was what the others called him. In every high school in his town there'd been, Norman remembered, a boy called Stick, a tall athlete whose brains resided in the fluid motion of his body. For boys like Norman, non-athletes but willing players, there had been no nicknames; boys like Norman had been only the background against which the more gifted ones could display their talents.

Every day for two weeks Norman went to play basketball in the afternoon. It was something to do, an excuse to leave the house, something for him to dream about in the City of Dreams. That is, when he wasn't dreaming about Heloise. Not so much the charms of Heloise, but the prospect of Heloise. Once, as he'd expected her to, she had even telephoned. It was during the morning, and when he answered she asked for Elisabeth — as though she didn't know that Elisabeth would be at work.

"And you," she said, "how are you finding Vancouver?"

"It's still perfect," Norman replied, surprised at the cool formality in her voice.

"That's good," Heloise said. And with those words her voice was back to the way it had been that afternoon in the kitchen — breathy, open, waiting for Norman to take the plunge.

Why not? Norman thought, why not now? "Let's go to lunch sometime," he could say. Or, "Have you any sights to recommend?" Or even, "Will the sky stay blue forever?"

But instead he made his lame good-bye and went down the basement to make sure he had two pairs of dry socks for basketball that afternoon. Bending over his laundry he felt a twinge in his stomach, a twinge he thought was a pulled muscle at first, but then, when he straightened up, he recognized as a familiar pre-boiling, a bubbling tension that used to start a couple of months before the end of one job and continue until the beginning of the next. "Phone her now," Norman said aloud. In the kitchen again, making himself lunch, Norman realized that the tingling in his stomach had actually started weeks ago, the afternoon he had first met Heloise Farraday.

He was slicing cucumber on a cutting-board he had bought at the health-food store. The board was red cedar, its flaming grain brought to a dramatic peak by several coats of oil. He took the moist slices and arranged them in piles. Each pile was a chapter in a junior creative-writing assignment. First chapter: the illicit meeting — accompanied by increased tension and feelings of pleasure; second, the illicit sex — tension to be replaced by pure pleasure; third, the disastrous dénouement — pleasure replaced by tension that increases until Norman loads up Nellie and drives to another city. Grade: C–. Comments: An idea too often repeated. Norman looked down at the cutting-board. The entire cucumber had been sliced away and now his stomach burned so much that he couldn't eat.

On the last day of the second week Norman noticed there was another stranger watching the game. He was wearing only khaki shorts and running shoes. He had glossy black hair that fell straight to his shoulders, and his skin was darkly tanned. "Paki," one of the players said right away.

Norman, running past the stranger, was uncomfortably aware of his stare. "If *you* can play," the stranger seemed to be saying, "then why not I?"

An hour passed. The stranger stood waiting to be invited.

"He wants to play," Norman finally said to Stick.

"Sure," Stick said. He beckoned the man forward with a tiny motion of his hand. Soon the new player was running up and down the court. But unlike Norman, he was in excellent condition. Every time there was a loose ball he was there, pouncing on it, dribbling it in a mad frenzy until he got to the basket where he hurled himself upwards and scored.

"Whirling dervish," someone said.

But no one passed the ball to him, nor did he pass the ball back. Soon it began to seem as if the stranger were a team of his own. Then, during a scramble for a loose ball, Norman was knocked to the ground. When he got up he saw the stranger racing down the court, his frenzied dribble carrying him straight to the basket. Norman brushed off his shoulder. His T-shirt was ripped and the flesh of his shoulder was scraped.

After supper Norman proudly displayed his wound. "The gladiator returneth unto his home and showeth his blood to the women who weep."

"You're crazy. I thought you were supposed to be working on your book." But that night, as Norman was falling asleep, Elisabeth opened the door to his room and joined him in bed.

Later, smoking a cigarette, Norman looked at the ceiling and said, "I have an announcement to make."

"The gladiator speaks. All fall silent therefore."

"You have to promise not to take it personally."

"Let the sword cut where it may."

"I feel good."

"You feel good?"

"I feel good. I hereby declare myself a member of the human race."

"You need a visa."

"You told me Vancouver was the City of Dreams and I laughed. I admit it. I thought you were just another Eastern convert to West-Coast boosterism. I thought I knew it all."

"You did."

"No, I didn't. I didn't know anything. Now I am here. Now I am lying on my back and looking at your ceiling. Now my muscles are sore and my flesh has been torn by honest exercise. I have just had sexual intercourse for the first time in months and my body is covered in miscellaneous fluids. I feel good."

"You feel good."

"And I have had a vision. Yea, after fifteen years or more or less of wandering in the desert. Yea, after more than a decade of having sand kicked into my face, camel dung dropped on my curriculum vitae, cactus needles stuck into the most delicate of my theorems, I have had a vision."

"Tell me your vision, master."

"I have looked into the mirror of the oasis, woman, and I have seen what I am not to be. I am not to be a mind slave, an intellectual, a member of the employed class. I am to miraculously become six-foot-three, superbly co-ordinated, and the best basketball player at the playground. And when this comes to pass I am to be known as Stick."

"Stick?"

"What surpasseth understanding shall be the bearer of Peace."

"But in this wasteland there is neither peace nor understanding. Only you and I, my lord."

"If I were your lord, I would marry you and make you happy ever after."

"But you are not."

"I know."

Saturday the blue sky turned milky with heat and Norman suggested he take Mona swimming. Once he was in the car, habit led him to the park. From his window Norman could see the players moving up and down the court.

Norman looked down at his feet. He was wearing brown lace-up moccasins that Elisabeth had bought him when holes appeared in his running shoes. The moccasins were made from caribou skin and had a strange musky odour. Flexing his toes, listening to the irregular staccato of the basketball against cement, glancing suddenly over at Mona who was sitting quietly with her hands folded and her eyes half-closed, Norman had a sudden desire to try to explain the hopeless logic of his life to her — the Nellie she was sitting in, the Nellies past and future.

On earlier wanderings he had found a special place, a sheltered cove with public access that he preferred to the larger and more crowded beach. Carrying a bag with Mona's things he helped her over the bleached logs until they reached the edge of the water.

Mona took her bucket and shovel from the bag and began digging furiously at the sand. Norman, meanwhile, lit a cigarette and looked out at the gently rolling sea. In the blue light the waves heaved up and down like a serenely obese belly. He undid his shirt, let the sun soak into his skin. After a while he closed his eyes and began dozing to the sound of water slipping in and out of the sand.

The night before, after Elisabeth had padded back to her own room, he had wondered if this summer in Vancouver was in fact the long-awaited exit from the desert — the resignation to his fate that would finally lead to release from bondage. He wanted to settle down; Elisabeth was available and even had a ready-made child. He wanted security; Elisabeth knew about a job in the English Department that had conveniently become vacant — a job that needed to be filled so quickly that there was no time for one of those competitions that drew hundreds of over-qualified wanderers like himself. Easy? What could be easier? Of course he would owe her. On the other hand she would be getting a husband, a father for her child. She had said she

wasn't for him — but surely she could be persuaded
otherwise, if only he would try to persuade her.

Persuasion, yes — although it wasn't persuasion
she was wanting: what she wanted, he knew, was
dedication, a proposition emanating not from desperation but from his own free will, from the part
of him she had written letters to, the part of him
that needed self-help. "Physician, heal thyself," she
had commanded; now was the moment for the
garments of doubt to be cast off, revealing the real
Norman Wadkins — lover, father and husband.

Then as night followed day the inner man would
propose to the long-waiting, long-suffering Elisabeth James that they combine in a Pact Against All.
Only in Pacts and Alliances could permanent escape from the desert be assured.

Norman imagined himself being masterly. He
imagined himself telephoning one of the babysit-
ters who advertised themselves at the Health Food
Bar. "I read your notice," he would say. "Would
you be free at seven this evening?" He imagined
himself with Elisabeth at a restaurant with tablecloths. Over wine, in the light of candles
moulded by Buddhist vegetarians, to the crackling
of burning logs and the hiss of breaking waves, he
would make his pitch. "Elisabeth, for heaven's
sakes, I've loved you this whole time. Let's drop the
pretences, darling, my heart is yours."

Just as he had fixed this perfect scene in his
mind, the actors began to change: instead of Elisabeth, Norman saw in front of him Heloise: Ruth:
the girl who had advertised her services in the
health-food store. The music played louder. Norman felt his heart beat faster. These were women for
whom he did not have to cast off the garments of

doubt. These were women who tore them from his back. These were women who could bring him brief moments of joy followed by months or years of unhappiness. "Norman," Norman said to himself, "these are the women you have learned to avoid."

"I want an ice cream," Mona said. Over the years she had switched into the first person. Norman stood up. As he was dusting off his jeans he heard a noise behind him. The stranger from the basketball court was sliding down the path. He looked briefly at Norman, no recognition in his dark eyes, then walked quickly down the beach and around the corner. Norman followed slowly. Beyond the small sheltered cove was a more inaccessible stretch where huge trees arched out from the last edge of land and hung over the water. In the shelter of those trees were a few huts and lean-tos where people had set up camp for the summer. Feeling like a spy, Norman watched as the stranger went to the first one and ducked inside. A few seconds later he re-emerged, an apple in his hand. Norman backed away before he was seen.

At the top of the path he met the other players. They were laughing, talking, smoking cigarettes. Stick clapped Norman on the back, the way he always did, then offered Mona a drag from his cigarette. She backed away, frightened. "Sorry," Stick said, "I didn't mean to scare her." Then he put his hand on Norman's shoulder. His hand was huge, the long fingers that held the ball so lightly now seemed almost inhuman. "See you Monday," Stick said. He had small even teeth, a smile that was like a blush.

When Norman and Mona got home, the Farradays were sitting in the living-room, a bottle of white wine had been opened, and the adults were laughing while the Farraday twins played with Mona's toys.

By the time the second bottle was empty, Norman had decided that if the bomb fell right that minute he might grab Heloise and take her downstairs to the safety of his basement bed. Then suddenly the Farradays and their twins had gone off taking Mona with them to spend the weekend at their cabin on the coast.

"I'll make some dinner," Norman said.

"Let's go out."

"My treat," said Norman. And then, unable to stop himself: "In fact, let's get dressed up and go to a restaurant with tablecloths."

Another couple of hours, another bottle of wine, and Norman found himself back in his dream of the afternoon. Only this time Elisabeth was with him and he was looking into her eyes, trying to feel love in the pit of his stomach. Or wherever. "The dream has come true," Norman considered trying. Instead he said, "You know, I finished the book revisions last week."

"You did? When?"

"Wednesday and Thursday nights. I stayed up late."

"That didn't take long."

"I guess basketball cleared my head."

"Are you going to apply for the job?"

"Un-hunh."

"Is that yes?"

Norman took a sip of water. "If I get a job, I'll have a salary."

"That would be one of the benefits."

"With a salary I could pay more rent."

"If it's not nepotism, it's bound to be corruption."

"Whatever happened to ordinary people, struggling to earn an honest dollar?"

"Us," Elisabeth said.

The waiter was standing above them. "More to drink?" Norman asked. "Coffee? Liqueurs?"

Elisabeth laughed. She had a smile, Norman suddenly noticed, like his friend Stick. Small and quiet, well-organized, the smile of generals who watch life fall into patterns around them. But no blush. "Do you want me to ask you to marry me?" Norman tried to imagine himself saying. But he couldn't say it. He couldn't even imagine it.

When they were in the car again, Norman put on "Your Cheatin' Heart" and with the music to encourage him drove towards the playground. He parked by the edge of the grass, turned off the motor. Through the open windows drifted the smells of late summer: water, grass, the city's exhaled heat. Nights like this he had parked other Nellies in random spots in other cities; cutting bonds, inspecting tires, running his hands over the steering-wheel and preparing once more to drive out blindly into nothingness. No, not nothingness, he corrected himself, but onto that long single highway on which the country's cities dangled, uncomfortably separated, uncomfortable at the prospect of each other.

Now he was gripping the wheel, stroking it. Elisabeth's hands covered his. He turned to her. *Now,* he thought, *now is the time to kiss her.* Then his thoughts sloughed away like old ice and he was bent over her, gratefully tasting on her lips the same wine that had passed through his own.

When they got out of the car they were still holding hands. It was a new experience, thought Norman, a sort of trial marriage. He led Elisabeth towards the little cove he had visited with Mona that afternoon. "I know a place where we could neck."

At first the moon lit their way, but when they got to the path the light was blocked by trees and they found themselves stumbling over stones and twisted roots. "The light at the end of the tunnel," Elisabeth said, just after a fallen log had brought them to their knees — but left them a view of an opening only a few steps away. Norman tried to imagine what Stick might reply if handed such a sentence. Perhaps, like an errant pass, he would simply redirect it to a more likely target.

The tide had gone out, the small beach of the afternoon was now a glistening expanse of wet sand. Still holding Elisabeth's hand Norman stepped towards the water. In front of the shelter he had seen that afternoon a huge fire was burning. The muffled sounds they had heard on the path now resolved themselves into excited talking and singing to the strumming of a guitar.

"Let's go over there," Elisabeth said. She tugged at Norman's hand and Norman reluctantly followed.

As they drew closer, Norman saw that all the basketball players from the afternoon were clustered around the fire, each accompanied by a case of beer. The stranger was the one playing the guitar; he had his eyes closed and he swayed back and forth as he sang.

"Look who's here."

"Just dropped by."

Soon a cold beer was pressed into his hand and Norman was talking to Stick and his girlfriend, a tiny voluptuous creature whose hair was an exact match for Stick's.

"Your boyfriend is a wonderful basketball player," Norman said.

"He was on the all-star team."

"Are you going to play at university?"

Stick shrugged his shoulders.

"He's working for my dad. He owns the semi-pro team. Then we're getting married in a few months."

"You are? That's wonderful." Norman leaned forward, smiling. He lifted his bottle to toast the event, and raising it to his mouth was aware suddenly of the absolute gravity of the bottle — its weight, its fullness, its cold perfection in containing the holy fermented liquid of communion. "Is this my second beer?' Norman asked.

"I wasn't counting," said the girl. She gave him a certain kind of look, a look filled with speculation and suspicion, a look which Norman had not seen for decades but now recognized from his high school years as the look residents give to tourists who are passing through. On their way to university and better jobs, Norman had then thought, but that was before he had gotten lost in the desert.

Norman stepped back from the girl. Beyond the crackling red light of the fire, beyond the slow moon-silvered waves sliding into the wet sand, he could see boats parked in the middle of the channel. Some of them were festooned and blazing, others had only a few identifying red and blue lights strategically placed. To be on a boat, Norman thought, to be riding the water surrounded by nothingness. Across the bay was a glittering stretch of apartment towers. And then, rising into the distance, the jagged silhouettes of the mountains.

His bottle was empty. He took another from a case that seemed to have appeared beside him. The years in the desert had turned him into a beer drinker but his body was unused to mixing beer and wine. As he swallowed he felt his stomach protesting. Another swallow, a more vigorous reaction. Stepping away from the firelight, Norman walked towards the bushes, looking for a place to be sick discreetly. He sat down on a rock, blearily drunk, and watched the channel boats rocking with the tide.

"With a salary I could pay more rent," he remembered saying. But Elisabeth had refused to rise to the bait: Norman staying, Norman leaving, Norman proposing, Norman failing to propose — she had cleverly contrived to leave it up to him. She had somehow become the sun that had simply to wait and shine while he, the planet, spun helplessly in her orbit.

Norman knew he was drunk. "I am drunk," he said to himself. Not because he had had too much to drink — although he had — but because he was trying to hide from the truth. From the truths. Truths that shone as bright as Elisabeth's sun. Other truths invisible and hidden black truths buried like hidden seams of coal. He was drunk, he was hiding and meanwhile meanings were waiting to be deciphered. Careful thought, textual analysis, semiotic deconstruction. These techniques — others too — were available and waiting for him.

As he had once explained to an indifferent class, the English professor is a surgeon who operates on the body of the text. Words were only on the surface — supporting them was a whole anatomy of structures, subtexts, themes, literary devices. And passion? Where did passion fit in? Passion was only a word, a concept, a single arrow in the large quiver. Or, on the other hand, perhaps it was a word that camouflaged other words — foolishness, youth, self-destruction. Unless on the third hand, the hand that wasn't, passion was all that mattered.

Norman let himself slide from the rock onto the more comfortable sand. The strumming of the guitar and the singing had grown louder. He closed his eyes and had a dim vision of the entire human race as over-excited water-bugs, each locked in its own shell, each in a frenzy over nothing. Then he thought of Mona. She was not a waterbug. She clung to his hand every Saturday and sometimes during the week. She laughed when he tickled her and cried when he wouldn't give her two ice creams in one afternoon.

There were the sounds of splashing, of gleeful shrieking as people dashed into the water. Norman stood up. He kicked off his shoes, stripped himself naked. Carefully he folded his clothes on a log then, still holding his bottle of beer, he advanced towards the sea. As he passed the fire he saw Stick's girlfriend look curiously at his naked body. Self-consciously he sucked in his stomach. He peered around for Elisabeth. Then he moved more quickly, first running along the wet sand, then straight into the water.

After a few steps the sand gave way beneath his feet and he was in over his head. Norman released his beer bottle and began to swim towards the boats.

It was years since he had gone swimming. But basketball had given him back his wind, and he felt powerful and strong as he sliced towards the centre of the channel. Then suddenly he was out of breath and gasping. He turned towards the shore. In front of the fire figures were waving—whether at him or at each other he couldn't tell. And then above the pounding of his heart he thought he could hear voices calling him. "I'm here," he shouted back. He was surprised at the loudness of his voice. He shouted again. He was treading water. The waves that had been so gentle when he entered the sea now seemed to be pushing harder, slapping against his neck and the side of his head. He decided to rest a moment, floating on his back. When he turned up to look at the sky, the water flowed over his eyes, into his mouth and nostrils. He began swimming again, towards the shore, but a current had gripped him and it seemed no matter how vigorously he swam, the fire was growing dimmer. Once more he rolled onto his back. Ripe clusters of stars hung above. "This is the way I want to die," he thought. He could hear music. His body would sink to the bottom of the channel, but his soul was flying into the white sky. He closed his eyes, surrendered himself to this final embrace.

When he woke up he knew right away he was in a hospital, knew right away that the face looking down at his belonged to Elisabeth, knew right away that the tears were coming from Mona. "I'll do a book on post-death experiences in modern litera-ture" was his next thought. He pictured himself sitting at his tenured desk, smoking filter-tip cigarettes and drinking a small glass of beer.

"Don't worry, I'm all right," he said. He was holding tightly to Mona's hand, he was crying and couldn't stop. Tears slid down his cheeks and the wetness brought it all back; they had hauled him out of the water and up onto one of the yachts. Wrapped him in a thick towel and given him something to drink. For a few minutes he had stood on the deck in the towel, looking at the shore and chatting as if the whole thing had been a humorous escapade. Perhaps the yacht belonged to Mark and Heloise, perhaps his shivering would stop when the warm flesh of Heloise was finally wrapped around him.

But Heloise did not appear. Nor Mark. It was strangers who surrounded him. Strangers who were looking at him curiously as he realized that nothing on earth could enable him to dive back into the sea and swim home. And he wasn't laughing, he was shivering uncontrollably. He had a first drink, then a second. Someone took him inside and he slid into a hot bath. The water burned at his skin but inside his muscles and guts were still frozen, still shaking uncontrollably, and even a third drink and a fourth didn't make any difference.

"I'm a doctor," someone kept saying. Norman looked up to see a man bending over him, a young rich-looking man of his own age with a friendly face and thick moustaches. "I'm going to give you a shot," he said from under the moustaches. And then the needle had entered his arm, a painful biting sensation that finally softened, sweetened, sent its sweetness and sleep humming through his blood until finally he was only aware that he was lying in the bath, enclosed by warm watery lips, floating in water, on water, the sky ripe and waiting above him.

When he woke up again Mona and Elisabeth were gone. He had a throbbing headache. He was wearing his own flannel pyjamas and a thick terrycloth bathrobe that belonged to Elisabeth. He thought about the book on post-death experiences. He would have to say how good it was, after dying, to be warmed and wrapped by the clothes of others. It made one feel part of the tribe again. It made one feel as though forgiveness was being offered.

In the pocket of his bathrobe Elisabeth had placed a note: "We love you, Mona and Elisabeth." The folded corners of the paper dug sharply at his palms, then he realized that even the air was clawing at his skin. Another after-death observation: "Upon their return to the world of the living, certain individuals are rendered hypersensitive. This manifests itself in reactions ranging from pure sensual pleasure to exaggerated feelings of terror."

When Mona and Elisabeth returned the next morning, Norman had prepared his proposal of marriage. "A Provisional Document Detailing Terms of Total Surrender" was the title, but before he could deliver it, he fell asleep.

His sleep was a transparent one. He saw himself lying on his back, hands stretched out to either side. Holding them were Mona and Elisabeth. They flanked him. They pressed their warm bodies against his so that he would be sustained. But Norman Wadkins was not dreaming. He was seeing, foreseeing.

He was foreseeing the future and in that brilliant future were man, wife and daughter.

In his mind the future was already the past. He had become a full professor, he had purchased new furniture for Elisabeth's living-room, he had converted the basement apartment into a combination study and sauna. In addition, he spent two evenings a week playing basketball for a semi-pro team. Not a front-line player, too old for that, rather a highly-strung specialist called into fill the breach, a pure shooter, a brief explosion of energy that might at any moment be seen skimming down the court, a blur among the slower, more awkward players. And then, when arms reached down for him, he was suddenly airborne, a soaring desert hawk: untouched, untouchable.

Remember Me to London

Remember Me to London

When she was young, Janis looked like a junior member of the Bloomsbury group: her blond hair was long and tangled, she wore once-elegant clothes that were beginning to unravel, and in photographs her large and intelligent grey eyes seemed to bulge forward, as if she was, even while the camera was on her, reading some impossibly righteous blue-stocking tract. After graduation she signed up for one of those six-week excursions down the Nile, with side-trips to the pyramids and other historical sites. "You who have stared into the face of the Sphinx," her friend Ellen Richardson called her in a letter posted to meet her at the Cairo Hilton; and Janis replied, "Mine eyes have rested on his visage and I say unto you that it is large."

By the time she arrived in Cairo at the end of her boat-trip, the strain of the tourist's existence had launched her body into a full-scale breakdown. The final days on the river, Janis spent cowering in her cabin, hiding behind the darkest of sunglasses. When the sun was in the sky, its blinding glare separated her from everything she wanted to see. And after it had set, when Janis was lying on her cot, blanketed by the heat and listening to the frenzied musical ribbons of the ship's orchestra, unwanted residues of the light exploded through her optic nerves, turning her entire cranium into a universe of igniting bombs and dull sonic booms.

The only way to soften the migraines was to drink; but then, just as she was beginning to enjoy this relief, the whisky sent her digestive tract some unwanted message and it responded in a violent insurrection against all forms of food except rice and mineral water.

From her Cairo hotel room Janis telephoned a representative of her travel agency. He arranged a semi-legal switch in her charter so that for only fifty pounds extra she could fly home two weeks later than planned — by which time she would have surely recovered.

Meanwhile, there was a diversion. Janis was in the bar, sipping mineral water and looking at a week-old copy of the *International Herald Tribune* when he sat down beside her. As she wrote to Ellen after the first night, in a letter she was never to receive: "I have met a certain fellow-traveller here, and I feel like a wicked woman about to blot my reputation. But why not? Here's to blots and passions, before the face that stared into the Sphinx falls off from old age and boredom." He was the perfect colonial type: he wore a tan suit and a white shirt; his tie was vaguely regimental; his cuff-links, gold, matched his watch and ring. The sun had darkened his face and lent a golden sheen to the tips of his brown hair; as he leaned towards her she couldn't help noticing the tiny white-bottomed wrinkles at the corners of his sympathetic dark eyes.

"You're an American, aren't you?" he asked. From the first time he spoke, Janis thought his accent was off-centre.

"English."

"I'm from New York. May I invite you to dine with me? In the hotel dining-room? Or anywhere at all, if you're feeling adventurous."

"No," she began, meaning to continue, "No thanks but I'm not eating"; instead she said, "I don't think I could eat here. What did you say your name was?"

"Mark Charlesworth," he offered. He sounded as thought he had learned his English at a Berlitz academy on another planet.

Before leaving she went upstairs, where she put on a black silk dress bought specially for the trip, a total extravagance that was high in the neck, in deference to what someone had told her would be wise in Egypt but clung suggestively to her breasts. She wrapped a lace shawl protectively around her shoulders and, just as she left her room, she swallowed two pills that the hotel doctor had guaranteed would put a definitive halt to stomach upset.

Stepping out of the taxi she tripped. Mark caught her and as she regained her balance, Janis felt a rush of panic at what might have happened, at the thought of herself lying face down in the street of a foreign country. The dining-room had a spectacular tile floor with a bandstand at one end. As they followed the maitre d' to their table Janis was aware

of her high heels clicking insecurely on the marble.
"You'd better have a drink," Mark said. His voice
gave her butterflies in the stomach, and when he
smiled she couldn't help noticing that his teeth,
very white, were also strangely irregular. She had
the unwanted thought that if he were truly an
American, his parents would surely have gotten his
teeth straightened.

In the darkened room, his disturbing white teeth
seemed to be the brightest point. While Janis drank
two martinis Mark kept the conversation going. He
talked easily about different countries, little anecdotes about being stopped in customs or marooned
in restaurants with inappropriate menus. Once he
mentioned a gift for a child, but whether the child
was his own wasn't clear. Perhaps it was an invitation to ask, but she didn't want to; she had already
decided that this night would be a one-night fling,
an excursion into the easy world of instant sex that
she had never truly entered. Even as the premoni-
tions of danger increased, she found herself beginning to giggle at the prospect of sitting in the pub
and telling Ellen Richardson the story. Every time
she spoke Mark's name she smiled at herself; it was
as if she wasn't even there, but was already watching the ragged movie of her adventure.

The menu was in Arabic and English. She let
Mark order for her, and when the food came she ate
heavily. Then they danced, cheek to cheek, on the
marble floor. The band was playing terrible imita-
tions of swing jazz; when she whispered that the
music was awful he loosened his hold. She looked
at him. He was grinning wolfishly. This was her
chance to end things before they got difficult, but
instead she moved closer to him, pressed herself

tightly against his chest though all she could feel was the rough texture of his jacket and the plastic buttons biting through the thin silk of her dress.

On the way back to the Hilton he held her hand but didn't try to kiss her. Then he invited her to his room for a drink. She accepted. They were standing in the elevator; it was only a matter of pressing a different button.

His room was exactly like her own except that there were two bottles of gin on the dresser. She had another drink, then stood up. Nothing was going to happen, she finally realized. Despite his sharp teeth and pointed alligator shoes, he wasn't a wolf after all, only a lonely man who didn't know the rules. "I'd better go. Thank you for the dinner and drinks." She heard her own voice wavering: what a pitiful sight she must be, she thought, a tarted-up and manless woman on a vacation from herself, from her boring and manless life.

"Please stay."

"I'm very tired. And I've had too much to drink." She wanted to cry. She was standing in the middle of the room; Mark hadn't moved from his armchair; she felt again the dizzying sensation of losing her balance as she had stepped out of the taxi. And then, just like in the movies, Mark leapt to his feet and folded her into his arms. She let him carry her to the bed. Somehow he managed to get the lights off without her noticing.

"The whole thing was actually very pleasant," she wrote Ellen, "not cheap at all. I expect he's a very nice man, even in real life. He says that he is American. He's got a lot of money but I don't see any guns."

Writing these words, which were not quite the

truth, Janis felt the excitement that comes from contemplating, at a safe distance, something very dubious. The truth she had omitted was her reaction to Mark Charlesworth. Because, also just like in the movies, the sex had been literally cosmic. All night they had made love; and Janis had felt like the last woman in the universe, floating through space, her body punctured by a million shooting stars.

The next night was a repeat performance, except that this time they had dinner in a restaurant which wasn't a hotel, and Mark explained that the child was a nephew who lived in Johannesburg. The second morning-after Janis didn't bother to write home; she might even have forgotten the total banality of her first letter had she not re-encountered it, unexpectedly, torn into shreds in the wastebasket of Mark's bathroom.

When she came out Mark was dressing in his tan suit. His straight black hair was moist and carefully parted on one side. He gave her his grin and saw her to the door.

She decided to go to the British Embassy as soon as she had showered and changed. But she found herself exhausted and instead spent the morning lounging in bed and reading a novel. After lunch she looked up the address of the embassy. She tried to imagine the conversation, her statement that she had found her own letter in the wastebasket of a man she had picked up in the bar of the Cairo Hilton. No doubt the consular officer would be young, wolfish in his own way, perhaps he would even invite her out for dinner. And meanwhile, what if Mark found out?

She had lunch alone in the hotel restaurant, an

excellent curry accompanied by a glass of white wine. Her stomach was cured, her migraines entirely gone. Reading the current week-old *Herald Tribune* she felt entirely content. It was only when she thought of going to the embassy that she was seized by fear. For an hour she sat in the lobby of the hotel, trying to work up the courage to step out the front door and take a taxi. In the end she went upstairs to her room, where she slept until Mark telephoned to invite her for dinner.

That night, in his arms, she finally revolted.

"What do you think you're doing?"

"What do you think?" he asked back, his voice pleasant and bland. He leaned over to kiss her and in an explosion of anger she pushed him away, then slapped him.

"Don't do that," he said, his voice still even. Then very deliberately he wound up and slapped her back, hit her so hard that she was knocked off the bed and onto the floor.

His hand had caught her across the ear, her skull was ringing, but Janis dragged herself up and pulled a pillow from the bed to cover her breasts. Mark reached out, took the pillow, tore it away from her in one easy motion.

"You stole my mail."

Mark nodded. Then he gathered up the bedspread and very carefully wrapped it around her. She shuddered at his touch. No one had ever hit her before. She was a big girl, almost as big as Mark. She had even taken a self-defence course. "I wanted to find out what you thought of me," Mark finally said.

"You—"

"I was afraid you would be making fun of me."

"You're crazy."

Mark shrugged. As always for their love-making the room was pitch black except for the yellow pool of light that spread out from beneath the bathroom door. "I'm not used to women. I didn't want to lose you."

"I don't believe you. I don't believe anything you've told me. Not your name, not your business. Not your nephew who was in Johannesburg two nights ago but in Paris tonight." With every word Janis felt new pulses of fear breaking through her skin. She had never looked for trouble with men. Now she was in exactly the situation she had always avoided.

"Do you believe that I love you?"

Janis didn't answer.

"I do love you." He leaned closer. He could kill her, she realized. Not just in theory but in fact. And then he could bribe the clerk who had intercepted her letter to mail her body instead. A tourist disappeared in Cairo? One who had overstayed her charter and had been travelling around town to different restaurants every night? Not the sort of thing that would cause a problem.

"I admire your courage," Mark now said. "I really do. Is it money? I was going to pay you at the end."

"You're not serious."

"You can have it now. Shall we agree on two-fifty a night? That makes seven-fifty." He picked his jacket from the back of the chair. "I suppose you won't take a cheque." He laughed and across his face flitted that same vulnerable look she had found so exciting during their love-making. "You're lucky. I have American money." He took a thick wad of bills and threw them to the floor. "Help yourself." And then, in an almost bitter tone: "I thought romance was part of the bargain."

"No," was all Janis could say.

"You can go now."

"Please. There's—" But she couldn't continue because the tears she had been trying to suppress now flooded out. Mark knelt on the floor beside her, his arms around her; his lips tenderly kissed the bruise on her cheek. Fear and doubt were equally mixed now, racing through her; then they turned to desire and she was kissing him back, looking for comfort in his arms, pulling away the bedspread so she could feel his skin burning against her own.

When they were calm again, and Mark was smoking one of his American cigarettes, Janis asked if she could see his passport.

He shrugged, then reached for his jacket. "I guess I owe you that."

Janis saw the name Mark Charlesworth, then beneath it, in smaller type, the names of his wife and two children. New York was given as his place of residence and of birth.

"What are you doing in Cairo?"

"I'm with a bank. The Chase Manhattan. I'm just an accountant, you see. I go to our different foreign branches, collecting figures. It's really very boring."

Janis looked at the money on the floor. It was a slowly expanding accordion of hundred-dollar bills.

He gave her his wolfish smile. "I'm like all bankers. I don't trust banks."

"I guess I'm like all girls," Janis said. "I don't trust boys."

"Trust me?"

"No." They were still sitting on the floor, between the two queen-sized beds that the Cairo
Hilton provided for the pleasure of its guests.

"I want to go back to my room now," Janis said.
"Will you let me go?"

"I love you," he said again. His voice was flat
and the words didn't seem to mean anything.

The whole time she was dressing he stayed cross-
legged on the floor, the bedspread pulled over his
lap, methodically filing the hundred-dollar bills
back into his billfold. Janis, straightening her hair
in the mirror, saw that her lips and eyes were
swollen. From kissing and crying, she couldn't help
saying to herself, and then imagined Mark Charlesworth's New York wife tossing in her sleep in her
New York apartment while she dreamt about her
husband's infidelities.

Back in her room she took a bath. The water was
cold but she stayed in it until she was shivering,
soaping herself over and over again. Ten days of her
vacation remained. She decided that in the morning
she would go to her travel-agent again and see
about changing the ticket.

She was still awake at four in the morning when
the telephone rang.

"I couldn't sleep."

"Me neither," Janis said.

"I can't sleep without you now."

"Soon you'll go home to your wife," Janis said.
"You'll be able to sleep with her."

There was a silence. Janis could hear Mark
breathing. She remembered Ellen complaining
once about a man who made obscene telephone-
calls to her from phone booths. It wasn't hard to

imagine Mark, in his tan suit, breathing heavily into the ear of a stranger.

"I think you're being unfair," Mark said. "You're a single woman on vacation. I invited you to dinner and you accepted. What did you expect?"

"I don't know. Not to be a prisoner. Not to have my mail stolen. Not to be beaten up." She remembered saying to Ellen that the first rule with obscene phone-calls was to hang up immediately.

"You hit me first." His voice was aggrieved, a little boy's voice. Janis placed the receiver back on the telephone. For an hour she lay waiting for the next call. Then she sank into a sleep full of jagged dreams. When she got up there was a note under her door; it was from Mark, inviting her to dinner that night. A gigantic vase of roses was waiting for her in the hall.

At the travel-agent's she tried to book a flight for Greece. The agent took her passport and made a telephone call. Then he returned and said that there were no flights available. That afternoon she went to the British Embassy. The man who met her was in his fifties, not at all wolfish looking. He made more telephone calls, then explained to her that the Greek air controllers were on strike and no flights were going into Athens.

"Of course your passport is good. You can go anywhere you like."

When she got back to her room Mark was waiting for her, inside. His attaché case was open on her desk and he was sitting in her armchair reading reports.

"How did you get in?"

"The maid let me."

"I could report you to the police."

"Janis, please, won't you talk to me?"

"I have nothing to say. Now please get out."

Mark stood up. "I have something to say. I'm sorry that I fell in love with you. I'm sorry if I'm acting crazy. You wanted to have a holiday, to relax, to have a good time? Why not have a good time with me? I promise to behave. I—"

"Get out," Janis tried to make her voice firm.

"You wanted to go last night. I let you go. You want me to get out now. I'm leaving. Why don't you trust me?"

You're crazy, Janis thought, but she didn't say it because he *was* crazy.

Mark snapped shut his case and put on his jacket. "Promise to have dinner with me tonight. We can eat in the hotel. You'll be perfectly safe."

"Get out."

"I'll be in the dining-room at seven o'clock," Mark said, as he swung out the door. "Wear your dancing shoes."

At seven-fifteen she went downstairs. It was, she had decided, a choice between meeting him there, where she would be protected by the presence of others, and waiting for him to break into her room.

When she got to the dining-room he was waiting, and beside the table was an ice-bucket with a bottle of champagne.

"I hoped you'd come."

"Then you must be happy."

"Have some champagne." He uncorked it himself, with crisp, expert motions.

"Thank you, Mark." It was the first time she had said his name since he had hit her, and at the sound of it coming out of her mouth she felt herself

stiffening with new courage. The movie had been
romantic at first, but now it was a spy movie, a
danger movie. She raised her glass. "You take the
first drink," she said. "Maybe you'll drop dead."

"Cheers." He drained his glass.

Janis sipped.

"I feel that we're on an island together, just you
and I. We're going to have a wonderful adventure."

"You're a real bastard," Janis said. "My mother
always told me never to trust Americans."

"I'm in the middle of a nightmare," she wrote to
Ellen Richardson that night. "I've never been so
frightened in my life. If I get out of this alive I want
you to show me this letter so I can laugh at it.
Meanwhile love, and remember me to London."
When she finished the letter she sealed the envelope, hotel stationery, and put it in her purse. Mark
had allowed her to go to her own room right after
dinner, and every few minutes she looked up to
make sure that the deadbolt was still in place. She
also rang the desk to ask for breakfast to be brought
at seven; at least her body would be relatively fresh
when they found it. She was fully dressed. Before
lying down to try to sleep she broke a glass in the
bathroom sink and put some of the shards under
her pillow so that when Mark broke in she would
have some sort of weapon.

At four in the morning she began to dial Mark's
room number, then hung up. She went to the
bathroom and was sick, but that increased her
terror instead of relieving it. As she was flushing the
toilet she thought she heard a sound in the corridor.
She switched off the lights, then lay face down on
the carpet and stared at the crack of light beneath
the door. There was definitely a shadow: Mark's

shoe? Another sickly-sweet love-note? A bomb about to explode in her eyes?

When breakfast came she was sitting in her armchair, dozing. The knock on the door thundered through her and even as she undid the lock for the busboy she could feel sweat pouring down the insides of her arms.

That day she went to the embassy again, determined to tell them about Mark. But the embassy was closed, due to some Egyptian national holiday she had never heard of. The travel agency was also closed. On her way back to the hotel she felt the heat and light beginning to invade her again, the way they had on the Nile. And as she crossed the lobby to the desk she saw Mark reading a newspaper. He sprang to his feet.

"Everything is shut down today," he said cheerfully. "Did you sleep well? You look tired."

"I have a headache."

"Let me take you to lunch. I know just the place. I promise you'll feel better."

"Mark—"

"They are friends of mine. A family. You must be getting sick of hotel food." His voice was gentle and solicitous. This must be, Janis thought, the way he talks to his wife after he beats her.

"My friends are Jews," Mark said. "Americans. Believe me, it's not easy to be a Jew in Cairo."

Janis contemplated the prospect of another terrified afternoon and evening in her room.

"You don't like Jews?"

"I love Jews. Just let me get changed and I'll be right down."

Samuel Isaacs was a bank employee like himself,
Mark explained, who had been posted to Cairo for
several years, then had chosen to stay on after his
retirement. To reach the Isaacs' house they took a
taxi across the city. Mark sat close to her, but not
too close, and pointed out the sights as they passed.
"I wish you'd let me take you around," he said.
"This is one of my favourite cities in the world."

The Isaacs lived in a palatial white house protected by enormous iron gates. Rachel and Samuel
Isaacs were the kind of perpetually youthful Americans Janis had sometimes met elsewhere in Europe:
white-haired, tanned, apparently infinitely rich and
generous. Rachel hugged Janis when they were
introduced and took her to the ladies' room to
"freshen up."

"Mark told me about you," she said. "I'm so glad
you decided to come to see us." And then, just
before they joined the men, Rachel Isaacs added:
"He never talks about his wife but believe me, it's a
terrible tragedy."

They ate in the courtyard, shaded by a colourful
umbrella. After two glasses of wine, Janis felt
herself beginning to relax. The air was warm and
honeyed, Rachel Isaacs was constantly attentive.
Samuel insisted on showing her souvenirs of Egypt
and explaining the origin and composition of the
food that the servants brought. He talked to them,
Janis noticed, in Arabic, and when he spoke they
nodded back respectfully without replying. The
hours slipped by, and as the afternoon began to
turn into evening other guests arrived, more Americans, and cocktails were served. As the shade
deepened Janis found herself drinking eagerly. She

got into a long conversation with a woman who had been an archaeology student, like herself. "This must be such a fantastic trip for you. I myself came here on a tour, just like you, and when I met John, he was working at the embassy then, I fell in love with the idea of staying. And him, too, luckily."

In the taxi on the way home, Janis let Mark put his arm around her. And when he took her to his room she didn't resist, only asked him to promise to be gentle.

"I promise," he whispered. "I would promise you the whole world."

That night he told Janis about his wife. Her name was Irene. They had met almost a decade ago, just after he had been taken on by the bank. She had been very glamorous then, very rich and very beautiful. He hadn't dared hope that she would be interested in him but she had allowed him to pursue her, and even accepted his engagement ring. After their marriage they'd had two children and everything seemed perfect until he found out she was seeing a lover. There was a terrible fight. Then Irene drove off in her car and had an accident. But it wasn't fatal; she'd been disfigured and partially paralyzed. Plastic surgery made her beautiful again, but in the process she became an alcoholic. Now she spent her life going in and out of clinics. The children lived with Mark when he was in New York, with his mother when he was away.

"So that's it," Mark concluded. "You see, I have very little to offer you."

"Why didn't you tell me earlier, instead of making up stories about your nephews?"

Mark shrugged. "It's not the kind of story you tell a stranger at dinner."

"And are there a lot of strangers? At dinner?"

"Some."

She lifted up his hand, kissed the tips of his fingers. "No wonder you carry so much money when you travel." She felt his hand stiffen, but only briefly. "I'm sorry, it's only that married men make me nervous."

For the remainder of her stay she slept with Mark every night. Twice more they visitied the Isaacs and, one afternoon when Mark was at the bank, Rachel took her to see some of the mosques. The morning of her flight she tremblingly packed her suitcase, absolutely certain it would explode in her hands, then went down to the lobby and ordered a taxi for the airport. The previous night Mark had said again that he loved her, and that he hoped he could be with her permanently some day. When he insisted, she had given him an address in London, but it was the address of her former ballet teacher, a woman who had long ago died. On the way to the airport, she was certain the taxi would be intercepted. Even while she was doing up her seat belt, she was sure that she was about to be shot; and when the 747 lifted into the air, she wondered if the hijack was going to happen immediately or after the cruising altitude had been established. When the plane arrived in London, Janis broke down on the tarmac. A sympathetic stewardess helped her through customs and told Janis that she herself never set foot outside the door of her apartment without a bottle of tranquilizers, just in case.

If You Have to Talk

If You Have to Talk

"To tell the truth," David's mother said, "I wouldn't have known she was French except for her Ess Ay—sex appeal, I mean."

In the mornings Marie-Yves used to speak French —little phrases, whole sentences, or sometimes only words for which she forgot the English equivalents until her cups of espresso coffee and a fistful of filterless cigarettes had rebuilt for her the bridge across the ocean and she was at home in Canada again, speaking English, as David's mother put it, "just like you and me."

After the blood tests had come back, David had stayed up all night drinking and brooding—saying only to Marie-Yves that he was finishing a script. When she came out to the living-room in the morning she mumbled at him and then, after some French that he didn't understand, said that she too loved her white nights.

David, far from finding this a digression, and for

the moment forgetting that in French "white night" meant literally a night illuminated, a night without sleep, was certain she must have discovered the truth. After that, breakfast continued as usual and it wasn't until six months later, lying alone and unable to sleep, that David's mind made the journey from white knights to white nights and back again.

In fact, at the moment his own white knights were entirely in disarray, though they hadn't always been. In that radically past other world of happiness and health, when David had been a little boy, white knights had been his white blood cells, coming to the rescue whenever some sickness put him to bed. "Close your eyes and listen," his mother would say. "Hear them coming, brave white knights in their thousands, galloping through your blood to fight off infection and make you well again."

Those were the good old days — the days when you went to bed and your white blood cells came to the rescue, instead of multiplying in some sick sexual orgy caused by nothing anyone, least of all the doctor, could modify. "Go ahead," she told David, when the results of the tests were finally undeniable, "get angry, throw things. Shout and scream. Decide you're immortal. That's the only way you have a chance."

"But I don't feel angry."

"You have to," the doctor said. Dr Sheilah Freedman. A young woman David's age: early thirties, dark hair, white skin sallowed by working too much. "Go home and have a drink. Have the whole bottle. When you want to get better, come to see me. I can help you, but you have to be ready."

"Some doctor you are," said David.

"Give me a chance. Maybe I'll surprise you."

"You already have, thank you."

For a while the rhythm of secret illness had dominated his life. But now, a year later, it seemed that the ringing of the telephone made the random dividing lines in his days and nights: the chirpy bird-like call of his study telephone, the hollow, limp-belled sound of the telephone in his bedroom, the solid-citizen clang of the old-fashioned wall telephone that had already been installed in the kitchen when he moved into the house. This time the voice was foreign, an unidentifiable European accent cresting through waves of static: "Marie-Yves Olivera, please."

"Marie-Yves Olivera no longer lives here."

"Thank you." And then the line was dead, despite the fact that he was still speaking, dutifully explaining that his ex-wife could be reached at her place of employment. There were other things that David could have told the operator. To begin with, that he needed someone to share his fear — why not her? Also that although he had kept his old telephone number, he had changed his house. Was now, indeed, residing in a place where his wife had never lived. Had visited only once, to be exact, in an unscheduled burst of heat — just a little action to initiate his bedroom and remind him that getting away is only a state of mind.

When the telephone interrupted him, David had been replacing the inner mouldings of his study window. He was back on the step-ladder, plugging some slack screwholes with plastic wood, when the telephone rang again.

This time it was Ivan; he liked to call himself

Ivan the Terrible, but he wasn't — just an almost eccentric lawyer with a talent for putting together film deals.

"It's good that you're home," Ivan said. "I wanted you to know that she's on the way."

"Who?"

"The researcher, you idiot. She's just your type, too. Fat, ugly and she can't cook. So you don't have to worry about compromising yourself."

"I told you to ask them to send résumés. Anyway I'm not seing anyone. Tell her to phone me."

"I'll leave that to you, since you're so charming. And by the way, the British deal went through. Another few months of sloth to pack away in your bank account."

Sitting on the highest hill of Ivan's rolling farm, looking down at fields picturesquely dotted with sheep and cattle, David felt a slight booming in his ears, as though a limousine were bumping its way along a dirt road inside his skull. He lay back on the grass and closed his eyes. *Limousine*, he had thought, not *hearse*. A sign of optimism? A mental lapse? Or perhaps something even more wonderful, a signal that for reasons even medical science could not name, his body had reasserted control over itself.

"David?"

"Here."

He sat up. A hundred feet below, Sheilah was picking her way through the junipers and granite boulders, zigzagging up the hill towards him. When she arrived she was out of breath, her cheeks crimson in the fall air, a thin bead of sweat across her upper lip. "I thought you were supposed to be sick." She dropped beside him, took his white hand between her two strong ones, rubbed it vigorously as though it was cold.

"I started running again last week."

"Good. Exercise kills toxins."

"Does it kill cancer, too?"

"We got the cancer, David. It's gone." Her hair so black, her white skin flaming, her dark eyes pinned on his — as though, David thought, suddenly angry, now that she'd saved him he was hers to re-make. Pygmalion with the sexes reversed. When her eyes dropped there was something timid, even passive, in the soft curve of her lashes. But like autumn leaves they mustn't be touched or else they might come drifting down to the ground.

In his dream Marie-Yves was talking to him. They were sitting in the living-room of the apartment they used to share, a big comfortable room with shabby furniture and an ever-renewed supply of fresh flowers. In his dream David was sitting in the reading chair; a pool of light illuminated the scarred coffee table where his drink, his cigarette, his unfinished script were huddled in untidy conference. "I suppose I should have told you earlier," Marie-Yves said. "It was one of those things. A sexual attraction."

Confessing this and after she wore a sweet smile.

"But weren't you satisfied with me? With our love life?"

"Oh yes. It was very beautiful. This other man, David, he had nothing to do with you."

He had nothing to do with you. These were the words she always said in the dream. In life, how-ever, things had been different. First of all, the unfinished script had been more than a decoration: to David it had been a symbol of hope — hope that he was successfully fighting the cancer, hope that if not, his script would give him a big enough payday to see him to the grave. Secondly, the light had fallen not only on his triangle of effects, but on Marie-Yves herself — her smooth tanned skin, the beatific smile he had always associated with their intimacy, the way her eyes held his without shame or denial.

"I could stay with you forever" were the words she actually delivered. "If you don't try to own me."

"Forever," David had repeated. Of course he had still not told Marie-Yves about the disease, though every night he meant to. But just after the diagnosis she had gone back to France to visit her family, and his first course of chemotherapy hadn't turned him blue or made his hair fall out. By the time she returned he was accustomed to not talking about it, accustomed to hiding his pills. And then the remission had begun so there were no more pills to hide.

"I love you," Marie-Yves said. "You love me."

"I love you. You love me." Those words were definitely from real life; he could even remember the charming way she had shaped her lips as she spoke, fine French grapes stretching out towards the sun, waiting to be kissed and forgiven. Which in real life had also happened: at least the kiss had. Instead of forgiveness, however, there was indifference. Indifference for a brief moment, then anger. Expressed first by hurling his script at her. Then by saying a few unforgiving and unforgivable things, coming finally to a climax when he announced that whether or not she stayed with him forever was an academic question, because six months ago he had been diagnosed as having leukemia.

"Leukemia?" As though it was one of those

arcane English words she had never encountered.

"Cancer," David simplified. It was the first time he had *said* the word.

Her eyes, round innocent cow eyes that he had always found attractive, now widened briefly, then assumed an expression at first puzzled, then horrified as finally Marie-Yves realized that not only was he telling the truth, but that his previous silence on the matter had forced her into cuckolding a dying man. This series of facial transformations was always the highlight of the dream, and it always took place in slow motion so that David could see the various layers of her deception peeling away until the final one was nakedly held out to him, the face of a woman convinced that what she had done wrong was not sleeping with a fellow worker, but committing adultery unnecessarily — by simply waiting a few months. . . .

In real life, however, the facial dance had whizzed by in record time, barely leaving David's subconscious a chance to record it. "You pig!" she had shrieked. "How dare you die without telling me! What do you think I am, one of your little students?" And then she had leapt at him, knocking him out of his faded paisley armchair and onto the floor where she punched and scratched at him until finally David let his fear crack open.

A moment of relief — then a long stomach-wrenching fall into the abyss which ended with him waking up in the darkness, soaked in sweat, a scratchy injured sensation in his throat as though he had spent the whole night begging for mercy.

"David is getting thin," Ivan said. "There's a theory going round that he's putting his sex drive into jogging."

"How far did you go today?"

"Yesterday," David corrected. "Five miles."

The idea had been to watch the sun come up and now, at the last moment before its rising, bars of light stretched from ground to sky, spiking into the sheaf of multi-coloured clouds that hung above the eastern horizon.

David was sitting on the floor of the porch. The heels of his shoes gripped the tongue-and-groove oak he had helped Ivan to sand down and refinish, and his back was wedged against the house, again on boards he had sanded and painted. Leaning against the wall, a blanket over his shoulders, he felt like a Mexican in a cowboy movie, the creeping light just now beginning to flare up from the ground to his face, illuminating his fine-boned silhouette beneath the broad-brimmed hat Ivan had insisted he wear for the occasion. All that was missing from the picture was one of those evil little cigars that movie Mexicans smoke, thin cigars that can be clenched between white teeth, removed only to spit out a few stupidly accented words.

Ivan was smoking such a cigar. This despite the fact that he was wearing no hat at all, only his newly frizzed platinum-blond curls that he called his Afro-punk halo. "People expect you to look crazy in this business," Ivan had explained. David had already made a mental note to buy Ivan, next Christmas — if he were still alive next Christmas — a gold chain with a matching crucifix. The possibility that he might not survive had shocked him into revising his note to say, also, that all the Christmas shopping should be done right away — though in fact he usually did none at all — so that his friends could remember him by the gifts his executor would distribute. For Ivan, the gold chain.

For Sheilah, a hope chest. For Marie-Yves, a one-way ticket to Graceland. For his mother, a treasury of dirty humour. He made the list and pinned it above his desk in the place usually reserved for his list of future projects. Sheilah had been the one to find it there and to worm out of him his exact plan. As penance she had prescribed the weekend at Ivan's farm.

Now Ivan was smoking his evil little cigar but David couldn't have one. Not a cigar or even a cigarette because Sheilah had also made him stop smoking. Other health-incanting measures: an alphabet of vitamins a day, exercise every two days, compulsory social life three times a week.

"David needs to get laid," Ivan said. "No one ever twisted their ankle making love."

"I had a patient last week who broke his toe."

"I could arrange it," Ivan offered.

"Like that researcher you sent me the other day. Did I tell you about her? Ivan said he knew a bright girl who was finishing her thesis and could look up a few facts for me. The next thing I knew this former Miss Winnipeg showed up on my doorstep. When she took her coat off I thought she was a strip-o-gram."

"Okay, I lied about the thesis. Anyway, I happen to know for a fact that Doreen has an I.Q. of one hundred and eighty-five."

"There's the sun," Sheilah said.

There it was. A yellow-white disc suspended above the ragged line of pine trees that marked the edge of Ivan's property. It burned weakly, like tea with too much milk, a fall sun diluted by the layers of mist which now began to shimmer and break apart.

Later Sheilah came into his bedroom. This was

new. Ivan had travelled with his current interest, an
extraordinarily intelligent camera assistant who
liked to go to bed early and sleep late; but though
Sheilah and David had arrived together, they assigned themselves their usual separate bedrooms.

"I want to sleep with you."

"Good. I'm perfect to sleep with. When I close
my eyes I'm gone."

"Cut the crappy jokes."

She stood in front of him wearing a flannel
nightgown: white background, small red and blue
dancing elephants providing the decoration.

"Did you hear the one about the elephant and the
cream cheese?" he asked as she slid under the covers.

"Just wrap your arms around me. If you have to
talk, tell me lies."

When David woke up the afternoon sun was
blasting through the thin curtain. Sheilah was
asleep, breathing in long slow sighs. Her elephants
were on the floor. David was curled around her, as
though they had been doing this for years. His
hand was on her shoulder. He moved it, looked at
the row of flushed marks his fingers had made. Her
skin was extraordinarily white. Marie-Yves's had
been darker, richer, and in the summer it had
turned the colour of sweet caramel pudding. But he
hadn't liked how she smelled — he had realized that
when they finally tried to make up in bed after the
night of confessions. She had a slightly overcooked
odour he had always been aware of but now for the
first time was able to articulate, the odour of having
spent too many hours sweating out love with too
many men, the odour of someone whose body liked
to crush itself against the bodies of others and suck
the sex out of those bodies and into its own pores —
like ground, needing to be rained on.

"So. Are you getting any?" This time the telephone had caught him when he was actually typing. Just before it rang he had been working the way he used to: record player turned up full blast, pitcher of coffee on the desk, fingers aching as he pounded out the dialogue.

"Pardon? Sorry, I couldn't hear you. I'll turn down the music."

"Are you getting any?" his mother repeated when he came back.

"That's what I thought you said."

"David, why don't you ever give me a straight answer?"

"I refuse to discuss sex with my own mother."

"What's wrong with mothers discussing sex? Am I past the age now? Don't I have my rights?"

"Can I call you back?"

"Can you come to dinner tonight?"

"I'm working."

"Sarah says she saw you with a woman at a movie last week."

An early November morning: Ivan's farm again. David could feel the hard-frozen earth kicking at him through the thick soles of his boots. He had woken up, the knife-dread fear of dying twisting through him again. Then gone out at the first light to walk himself sane. Now he was following a small quick-running stream through a steeply banked maple grove. The branches made a thick naked tangle in the grey air. On the ground was a light dusting of snow — just enough to reveal the tracks of chipmunks, rabbits, even birds. David knelt at the water's edge, picked a transparent piece of ice from the shelter of a small rock and sucked at it. The cold water ran between his teeth. Ice juice.

He put his hand in the water. In a few moments the feeling of flesh was gone and he was aware of the current tugging at his fingerbones as though to carry them away.

By the time he got back to the farmhouse the sun had burned itself an opening in the sky and pocked the snow so that the white fields were mottled by wet green grass.

Ivan had gone to town for groceries, but Sheilah was sitting at the table going through a stack of medical journals. In her owlish reading glasses she looked absurdly young, fragile. Watching her through the window David imagined himself in the kitchen, silently walking behind her and bending to kiss the warm white skin of her neck. Then the dread sharpened from simmer to boil and he imagined himself out of the picture, out of the room, out of everything. When he went inside, Sheilah got up to embrace him. A gesture so surprising that he stood without moving until in the tight squeeze of her arms he could feel her heart against his chest. And then looking over her shoulder at her magazines David saw that she wasn't reading about him after all. Other people, other diseases.

Of course he had told neither his sister Sarah nor his mother about the cancer. "You have to tell people," Sheilah argued. "Hiding it from your family is just a way of hiding it from yourself." She recited the words as though they were being quoted directly from one of the textbooks for which she had such an amazing memory.

"You said I was cured."

"You're in remission, David. Nothing lasts forever."

After a while he began to notice that he was growing thinner. Lying in his bed, he seemed to take up less room, and when he saw himself in the mirror he was constantly watching the way his ribs were melting the fat around themselves — first emerging as little Jacob's ladders, then seeming to grow right out from his sides.

"You're bony," Sheilah said one night. "If you're going to do all this exercise, you'll have to eat more."

But he wasn't interested in food, wasn't interested in anything except melting his flesh away before the cancer could attack it. But before he made his escape, there were still a few things to take care of. "Your mother," Sheilah said to him, the day he went below a hundred pounds, "If you're going to starve yourself to death you ought to tell her."

"I talk to her on the telephone all the time."

"And she thinks your voice is fat?"

"I'll write her a letter."

Dear Mother,
After you receive this you may not hear from me for a while. I have decided to move to Philadelphia where I am taking up a teaching position at a university for young women. Please don't worry about me; it has an excellent reputation for hygiene.

While I am gone it is possible you will hear terrible rumours. Even, excuse me for saying it, rumours that I am dead. Please pay no attention to these. You know that my producer, Ivan Youngblood, is willing to do anything to attract publicity. He has a doctor friend, Sheilah Freedman, who connives with him on many of his schemes. After three years, if you haven't heard from me, it may be time to reassess the situation. Until then I remain, as always, your faithful son.

"All romantics meet the same fate" were his favourite words from the song. Played top volume counter-blasting the sticky Toronto heat. Taped to the wall was the letter David had written — but not mailed — to his mother. Underneath it was taped a strip of paper saying: "Old Chinese proverb: the story of a dying man always ends in death."

But he wasn't dead. He was typing, and the noise of his machine and the music were almost enough to drown out the fear and the sound of the telephone. Which wasn't ringing yet but would be soon, bringing Sheilah, Sheilah's voice, the results of the latest tests. Tests on Sheilah, this time, to see if their combined project — now in its embryonic stage — was going to be a moron or otherwise afflicted.

He was typing fast, hitting the keys hard enough to make his knuckles ache. He was writing the outline for a new script, to be called "White Knights/Nuits Blanches," the story of a cancer-stricken writer whose doctor makes him exercise until he starves the cancer away. A sentimental story with a surefire happy ending, guaranteed money in the bank for the next generation. But the harder he typed, the worse he felt, and by the time the call came he had stopped working, turned off the music, and was lying on his back on the floor, staring up at the ceiling, trying to remember if there had ever been anything other than this deep roaring silence that was exploding from the centre of his heart.

The Bone Fields

The Bone Fields

"In the harmony of spent light, words are reborn."
So Stigson begins tonight. Keeping us warm are
thick chunks of maple burning in a place we call
the theatre. Not a building but a small meadow
backed by a curved rock wall.

Against this wall we sit.

Off the rock bounce heat and light, keeping us
warm, illuminating our faces, giving us the slowly
dancing shadows of giants.

"I could tell you the story of the man who
became his own dream," Stigson offers.

Silence.

Stigson moves closer to the fire. He is a big man
and his face is large even for one of his size. A
largeness accentuated by his beard. When I became
Stigson's follower his beard was a luscious corn
yellow. Now it is the colour of corn leaves turned
brown and streaky by frost and cold rains.

"You," Stigson suddenly calls out. Without Stigson we cannot live. "You," he calls again. He is looking at no one in particular. He is looking at everyone.

Annie stands up, stumbles forward. Has Stigson singled her out without my noticing? Has the whole scene been prearranged?

Annie stands in front of the fire, her arms folded. Stigson towers over her.

"What can you offer us tonight?" Stigson asks. His voice sounds dangerous. More than usual? I ask myself; or is it only that I am always thinking that Stigson grows ever more virulent?

Annie looks out at us. I can't see her face. She seems to be shaking. On a night like this a year ago Annie's brother was selected in the same way. By the time morning came he was dead. Did Stigson kill him? Did everything I remember really happen? It must be true. That is, when I remember how to find a certain lake, a certain cache, a certain path through the forest, the lake, the cache, the path are always waiting for me when I arrive. So too, therefore, what Stigson has done. Except that death, ecstasy, even boredom are not places that can be visited. Just the memory or, in the case of death, the body. Certainly the part about the body is true. I dug the grave myself. Myself lifted Edward up and dropped him into the earth. He was heavy, I remember thinking, the real and substantial heaviness of life was still in him. Though in fact he was stiff with death. Even when his body thumped to the bottom of the grave his muscles and bones rigidly held their position. Knees bent. It was said that Edward had spoken against Stigson: dissent, jokes. Never to me, of course, because I above all am supposed to belong to Stigson. "My Judas," Stigson once went so far, meaning what I don't know because I am no Judas, Stigson no Christ, and besides — all those who would have been Romans died long ago.

Annie reaches into the pockets of her coat and her hands emerge cupped to overflowing. Stigson grins. Our fear turns to excitement. The script was planned after all — Stigson taketh away but Stigson also giveth. One by one we come forward. Under Stigson's watchful eye we swallow our portion of the mushrooms. Kettles are hung over the fire. While waiting for the drug to take effect we drink hot tea and dream our adventures of the night ahead.

Two small frogs sitting on a log. This was a long time ago, the summer I was ten years old. The log was a recent arrival: a storm had blown it down the lake and now it was resting in the lee side of our absent neighbour's dock. Stigson was a year younger than me, but bigger. Thick straw-like blond hair that spiked out from his round skull, blue eyes that begged to be lied to, largish ears perpetually sunburned. We were wildmen that summer. Stigson had been placed under my command by his parents. We had uniforms: sunbleached jeans, shrunken T-shirts, white canvas sneakers with holes worn in the little toes, battered men's fedoras circled by greasy black bands and adorned with birdfeathers. I had twenty-two feathers, Stigson eighteen. At the beginning of the summer I had assigned us ranks — I Captain, he Sergeant; but with each new feather a promotion was required so I was now Admiral of the Galaxy,

Third Degree, whereas Stigson, owing to a stretch of bad behaviour, was stuck at Solar System Commander.

Stigson and I were in half-uniform — jeans and hats, lying bellies-flattened on the dock. The frogs were the dark green of the underside of oak leaves. They longed to jump into the water but they didn't dare. They had been sitting still so long that their pores were turning into volcanoes. They knew that Stigson and I were watching them; perhaps they had even smelled the dead feathers in our hats. Like soldiers, I thought — that summer was my military history phase — at the edge of some ancient bloodied battlefield, too frozen with fear and dread to save themselves.

Stigson looked at me. Our fishing rods were on the beach, baitless hooks hungrily dangling on the sand.

One of the frogs breathed. Its underthroat fluttered in the stillness. Silent, silent, Stigson and I wriggled forward. It had taken us forever to inch across the dock. A forever of iron discipline, of exchanged looks, of breath breathed with the changing breeze. Now we were at the dock's edge. We were curving our bodies so that our shadows would not be visible to the frogs. We were about to fall into the water — this was a trick we had practised earlier in the summer, a similar occasion; as we slid through the air, but before our bodies made a splash, we would clap our hands over the ambushed frogs.

I nodded to Stigson. Silently we rolled off the dock. Our hands came down like guillotines. As the cold water shrunk my skin I felt a wild struggling under my palm. The water, the sudden sun in my eyes, the sound of Stigson whooping in triumph, the live being insanely squiggling to escape my grasp. I squeezed tighter. The frog was dry but gummy. I slid it into the water. It relaxed, its skin expanded into its normal happy slime, it began to hope I was only playing a cruel but temporary game. I didn't want to know what the frog was thinking, but I did. I decided to order Stigson to let his frog go. But he was already on the beach, digging his barbed hook into the prisoner's lower jaw, running at top speed towards the shaded grass knoll from which we were going to offer it to the big bass we knew was waiting in the deep shaded pool below.

It was early morning. The sun had turned the sky atomic blue. Stigson and I had spent the whole summer inventing this strange planet. My hat was floating at my knees. In my hand wriggled alien life and above my head a hawk scribbled a message I had just learned to decipher.

Lying in the forest blackness. Most of my body has melted into the cold earth. Only my brain is alive. Fluorescent, glowing ghostly white, it floats through the forest. "Go," I say. Soon it is working its way up through the leaves, towards the sky, finally it is in the clear and accelerating towards the moon.

Leaves rustle. The air is heavy and cold.

I listen to the earth's heart beating.

In my empty skull, acorns take root, twin oak-trees shoot through the sockets of my eyes.

This morning I shaved. Looking into the cracked mirror of a long-dead pickup truck I scraped away

my stubble. Amazing that in only a week you can
forget your own face. Mine always surprises me by
looking so young: cheeks, chin, lips — all smooth
and unmarked. The face of an executioner I would
once have said. But now there is almost no one left
to execute. All of us here — in Stigson's group and
in the whole area — belong to the Vegetarian Cult.
At least officially. In any case none of us (except
perhaps Stigson) would ever kill a person. Even an
animal. But fish are allowed because, Stigson
decreed, fish do not dream. Dreams are what is
sacred, Stigson went on, because dreaming is life.

Life, lifespores. It was one of the first times on
mushrooms that I had the vision of Life. Lying on
my back — like this — damp ground and fallen
leaves trying to melt into my skin — like now, I had
been afraid that I was dying, that I had already died
and forgotten my life, that my body was rotting
into the forest floor. Unable to move, melting into
the cold soil, I closed my eyes. In the midst of the
darkness an explosion of light. Otherworldly music. A storm of dancing molecules whirling
through space, combining and re-combining,
changing shapes, configurations, loyalties — a
storm of random possibilities colliding into each
other until the magic combination was achieved
and BINGO — a living being.

Stigson's father was a doctor, but he preferred to
call himself a physician. "My father is a *physician*,"
Stigson would announce solemnly when I introduced him to the children of other cottagers. Stigson, a city boy, was deemed to need my bit of
country gloss, which was why he was put under my
care. Stigson's father, the *physician*, was rich. Their

cottage was a split-storey wonder which had a sandy-beached bay to itself. Like other doctors, even those who did not call themselves physicians, Stigson's father could paint on iodine, sew stitches, prescribe pills and ointments. And then, the week of the "accident" at the Chalk River heavy water plant, Stigson's father was called away. To cheer up Stigson I gave him two extra feathers for being a temporary orphan.

"He does radiation sickness," Stigson offered one morning. We were on one of our fishing expeditions, an hour's hard paddling from Stigson's boathouse where the canoe was kept.

I knew what radiation was. Deranged molecule and atom parts, little overcharged matter-bullets, unbalanced micro-psychopaths careening tribelessly through the universe.

From his fishing tackle-box Stigson drew a plastic vial of pills. "These protect you," he said. "My father gave them to me." He scooped a handful of water from the lake, messily swallowed two tablets. He offered me the bottle. "Go ahead."

It was August. A summer day on the lake. Glassy wrinkled water. Granite cliffs that could scorch your hand. Centuries-old pine carving the bone-blue sky.

"I have a thousand pills hidden in secret places," Stigson said. That was true, I found out years later. Only by then the thousand had become tens of thousands, buried in hiding places all over the countryside, caches that Stigson, while I was supposedly teaching him, had memorized so well that even decades later he will suddenly exclaim over a remembered configuration, push into the woods through thickets that would not even have existed at the time, move aside rocks, fallen logs, an apparently random stone in the side of a hill and come up with another of his precious plastic vials.

"You'll die if you don't," Stigson said.

He was ten years old. Spiky blond hair that tapered into arrows when he swam. A bridge of freckles over his nose. A mouth that was always a bit open showing large milky teeth. A babyish looking boy, I had thought when first introduced, looking so young and so fragile that instead of feeling I was finding a playmate I thought I was being given a babysitting job. Wrong. Because Stigson, though younger, was already stronger, smarter, quicker. But most impressively: always in perfect control. For example, after he first defeated me in a running race I took him in the canoe and made him keep paddling to my pace, wanting to force him to give up. That day, early in July and the sun shining like a knife off the water onto Stigson's pale back, I watched him match my every stroke while the skin on his back turned first pink, then a bright angry red along the bony ridge of his shoulders. Until it was I who stopped. I who suggested that we beach the canoe. I who slipped into the water to relax while Stigson, bright-eyed and curious, watched from the shore. Waited until I had floated out towards the middle of the lake and then he got into the canoe and made as if to paddle away, leaving me to swim home or walk back barefoot around the edge of the lake.

"Swallow," Stigson said. He offered me a pill, our first communion.

I swallowed. We didn't die. Nobody died except for two nuclear technicians at Chalk River and those deaths were hushed up.

Mynor Jones's face looked like a baked potato left overnight in the oven. The skin was mottled and grey. Baggy, layered, and crumpled. One ear was turned out to catch the wind. A large donkey's ear with a hanging lobe discoloured by annual frost-bite. The other ear, wise and/or timid, lay close to the head. Most often it was covered by Mynor Jones's lank black hair.

When he leaned towards you — possibly over the table, possibly across a fence or stall partition — you saw the timid ear ducking for cover behind the greasy black veil while the social wind-catching ear hove forward.

"I'm the old man in the ark," Mynor Jones liked to say. He lived in the house where he had been born. Slept in the bed where he had, according to himself, squirted like a rocket from his mother's womb. "I'm still living," he repeated ten times a day. It was true. Mynor Jones lived, while all the other locals — farmers, storekeepers, even the drunks — had died from radiation poisoning. "Newcomers," Mynor Jones explained. According to him, and there was no one left to contradict him, his family had been the first to settle in this particular little valley. Sent over from Scotland with the promise of railway lands, Mynor Jones's great-great-grandfather had somehow gotten off at the wrong stop, become mixed up with a group of fur-traders, found himself eventually being pensioned off with the land grant of a farm which, it turned out, existed only in the imagination of the man to whom Mynor Jones's great etc. grandfather had paid all of his cash plus two bottles of bad whisky.

"He hacked and he hewed," Mynor Jones said.

When we were out cutting with our own axes, Mynor Jones was always boasting that the original Jones could have done whatever we were doing in half the time and half the sweat. "My ancestor could take down a tree like this in ten minutes," he would boast when after an hour we were doubled up panting while the tree remained perfectly straight, nothing to show for our efforts but a ragged V-notch halfway through its trunk.

Last year Annie and I spent two full months hiding at the farmhouse of Mynor Jones. Full moon to full moon to full moon. We stayed in what had once been called a summer kitchen, was now a junkshed with a rusting wood stove and a mattress. Stigson was too proud to come looking for us. For Jones we cut wood, cleaned house, baked ourselves at his makeshift forge trying to turn the remains of his various tractor implements into hand tools. One week I made three shovels. Not bad. And carved a dozen hickory handles while sitting by the fire, my knife digging into the wood and Annie's hot vegetable soup boiling in my guts.

"Now this is the life," Mynor Jones said. "Why don't you two pill-takers just settle down here?"

Mynor Jones had whisky. Two years old, aged in various kegs he kept in basement and barn. The recipe for Mynor Jones's whisky: a gallon of last year's batch, a few more gallons of well water, add hand- or basketfuls of every fruit within a mile of the house until squishy, fill to the top with more water or juice and cover until ready for extinction.

Annie wouldn't touch the stuff, but sometimes I stayed up late with Mynor Jones in the kitchen, keeping him company over a gallon jar. "Might as well save the candles," he would say. If there was a moon, the white light reflected off the snow would create a ghostly glow bright enough to throw shadows, to deepen the hollows of Mynor Jones's face into trenches, to turn his mouth into a deep well. Light enough, too, so that afterwards when I buried my head in Annie's belly I could open my eyes to warm curved marble. But in that moony glow her lips and tongue were the colours of death, her eyes flat.

"Take me away, Annie," I would whisper. But Annie wasn't taking me anywhere because Annie was gone. Except sometimes, sometimes — sometimes in the middle of the night there was Annie stoked up like a furnace, Annie burning a full head of steam, Annie on fire, Annie in heat, Annie waking me up full of craziness and desire.

When we came back Stigson gave us the look we were usually spared and said, "I thought you were dead." In those two months, I thought, he had aged two decades. But with summer he filled out and gained strength again, his own theories always working best on himself, bouncing back higher the lower he sank, always the surest, the most confident, the most powerful.

Once we were tens of thousands. An amazing coincidence, I had thought, that the area where I had spent my boyhood summers was one of those best suited for survival. But then Stigson explained it was no coincidence at all, that for two years his father had studied the patterns of wind, rock and vegetation most resistant to radiation. This region of eastern Ontario was, Stigson said, geologically speaking, one of the most primitive in North America. Pre-Cambrian rock hundreds of millions

of years old. Limestone made up of billions of
prehistoric sea creatures. Even the lichen we used to
start our fires had been growing for hundreds of
thousands of years.

The more of us alive, the more there were to die.
By this time Stigson had more pills, better pills. In
those days different cults often collided with each
other in their foraging. And in those days, too, the
skies above the bone fields were sometimes black
with crows coming down to feast on irradiated
flesh. "Microwave meals," Stigson would sneer. In
those early times Stigson would give sermons about
how the past had been turned into the future, how
the world had been driven to suicide by fast food
and television.

That was when Stigson's father was still alive. He
had his own theory — which was that all along
there had been subtle evolutionary changes preparing the species to weed itself out using this catastro-
phe. Pills or no, he insisted, some of us had already
developed body chemistries to cope with radiation.
Just as the population was already being trimmed
down by cancer, AIDS, epidemic starvation, he
pointed out, before this latest disaster. Only one
remaining problem: evolution needed a quantum
jump, a mutation of the species, a blast into the
future. What better blast than massive doses of
radiation — eliminating some while creating new
genetic peaks for mankind?

So that was his vision — a species-wide transfor-
mation kicked off by atomic disaster. And one day
near the end I gathered up my courage and asked
Stigson's father why it was we needed to change.

He was lying in bed, a massive bearded man gone
to big-boned skeleton and hanging flesh, matted

salt-and-pepper beard hiding the sores which had begun to infect his face.

"What do you mean 'why'?"

"Why did we need to change? Why not go on as we were?"

I expected an outburst on the moral cruelty of man, his evil towards himself and other species, his inability to live naturally among the birds and the flowers. Don't ask me why, but I had always thought this was the direction in which Stigson's father's mind was turned. "Other planets," he croaked. "Flying saucers, creatures from outer space. Where have you been all these years?"

"Here."

"Exactly. We should have been in space ten thousand years ago. That's why we destroyed our own planet. We were stuck on it. Glued by our lack of evolutionary change like overpopulated rats in a cage. Everyone knew that. Everyone knew we had to get off. But how? We lacked the —" He coughed, started jabbing at his head with his forefinger.

"Brains," I said.

"No, idiot, imagination. Evolutionary motor. We lacked the chromosomes. Every religion in the world believed in original sin — one way or another, believed in personal guilt, when the real problem was our chromosomes. Scientists began understanding that what we needed was not moral rearmament but a biological boost. It was another version of the old missing-link problem. So if the link was missing, it was up to us to create it. Some tried to manufacture it in a test tube, others worked on altering the chromosomes of potential parents —"

"And others," Stigson completed for me the

night after his father died, "decided that the best
solution was at once the most radical and the most
democratic — a proliferation of apparently
'random' nuclear accidents that would allow the
human race to be reborn at a higher level. Of course
there was no plot, no actual conspiracy. Just the
circulation of an idea informally discussed at various international conferences. At first the accidents
were tiny. The public always blamed them on inept
bureaucrats or patronage construction. But scientists knew the Three Mile Island disaster must have
been caused by human error. Deliberate human
error. To show their goodwill, the Soviet scientists
created Chernobyl. Then came Chalk River. A
couple of years later there was the 'accident' in
India. After that things began to get out of hand.
Like lemmings, you might say."

The bone fields began as the idea of another cult.
Stigson's father, still alive, was in favour. No good,
he said, burying the bodies in the usual way.
Radiated corpses lying in the ground, exuding their
half-lives for tens of millions of years. Better using
the huge limestone quarry lined with thick layers of
cement by those still alive at the time who knew
how to do such things and had the necessary
equipment.

   And so it was, at the beginning, that the dead
were driven to the site and dumped. Those were the
early days when fuel, cars, civilization seemed destined to limp on for decades. In those days, for
example, it was still possible to believe Stigson's
father and his friends might have known what they

were doing. Possible to believe that somewhere in some unsuspecting belly the new race for the new age was ripening, the evolutionary step humankind had awaited for millenia.

Now small mountains of crushed stone encircle the bone fields. The graders and bulldozers are parked in the midst of these mountains, permanently stationed guardians frozen forever when their gas tanks went dry for the last time.

When the task of burying and covering echoed through the countryside every day, the sky above the bone fields was often black with crows and vultures. Now occasionally a lone crow with a long memory circles above. All it finds is more memories. These days the dead are buried where they drop.

But still I am attracted to the bone fields. Sometimes, perched on a gravel hill or sitting behind the wheel of an old rusted grader, I'll see the others, from other cults, making their own visits. We are the survivors, whether because of our chromosomes, our pills or pure chance is unknown to us.

In summer the whiteness of the bones can be tinged with yellow.

The light of autumn sunsets turns them darker.

Rain drains away quickly. Even snow tries to melt on contact.

Back from moon, from sun, from stars. What have I brought with me? A memory, perhaps an image. A scene from a movie that will never be made. The engine of the universe, the universal engine. Beads of yellow-white electrons dancing, incandescent particles exploding. Clouds of isotopes drifting through nothingness.

Radiate
Radiate
Radiate the food you ate

Put it down
Throw it up
Drink out of a glowing cup.

One two
Three four
All we ask is one more war.

Stigson says ours is a generation of guardians. We have survived. We survive. We hold the earth in trust for those to come.

Foraging but not killing
Cooing but not billing

Journeying into our nighthearts to touch the centre, fuel the fire.

Some day, Stigson says, we or our children or our children's children will see the dawning of the new consciousness. For now we are in a tunnel whose end is only the light of our fragmented memories. We are, Stigson says, Plato's savages in the cave, but when we or our children or our children's children emerge, it will be forever.

I am lying on the forest floor, back from the moon (the stars, the nothingness), my skin like a sponge soaking up lifespores from the earth. Stigson will still be by the fire. Not now, but soon, he will come searching for me. Stigson is bigger than I am, faster, stronger, smarter. But tonight Stigson will not find me because I am afraid.

Guardians, Stigson calls our generation. He invents history as he needs to — past, present, future are the cords he uses to enslave our minds.

Not mine, I like to think.

I am no guardian.

I am the survivor who mistakenly survived.

After us there will be no one. We are the last. When we are gone, the planet will continue its slow circles around the sun, its pierced ozone layer will commence the multi-million-year process of healing, trees will gradually push their way through broken pavement. Finally the planet will either heal itself or not, become green again or collapse from its self-inflicted poisons.

I blame no one and nothing.

To blame is to say things might have been different, that if we humans had played our cards right we could have enjoyed the Garden of Eden forever. I stand up. I wrap my arms and legs around my favourite oak-tree, sink nails and teeth into its understanding bark. Then jump down again. Time to start sliding — through the woods, away from Stigson, away from the fire.

Half an hour and I am at the edge of the lake where Stigson and I played our childish games. At the sandy shore a thin skin of ice. Waiting for me, where I hid it, is a canoe. Quietly I slide it across the frosty sand. In the bushes the paranoid rustle of a porcupine. The ice breaks under the canoe's weight. I hopscotch a few rocks, step into the canoe. How I love the tug of water against paddle, the sensuous lick of the lake on varnished canvas. In the woods the night air was thick and green, full of resin and dead leaves. Over the water the air is cooler, purer. Soon, from across the water, I will be able to smell the open earth of Mynor Jones's tilled fields. Perhaps even a dry curl of woodsmoke. Like the ionized colours of the twilight sky, so too the last smells of the dying planet.

I put my paddle across my knees. Tiny streams of water flow off the wood and make their silvery sounds as they splash back into the lake like miniature bells. I plunge the paddle in, draw it out, just to repeat the sensation.

From the south shore a sudden staccato of coyote yips. Lately it seems they've been dying, though no one ever sees their bodies. "They bury themselves," Mynor Jones insists, as though they can dig their own graves and then pull earthen roofs shut over top. But necessary details do not interest Mynor Jones. He knows what happens. How it happens is for other people — people from cities perhaps, the kind of people who commit mass suicide — to figure out. "Where there's a will, there's a way" is as far as he's willing to go. And then adds that when his turn comes, he intends to do the same.

In early October there was a sudden plunge from Indian summer. Two nights of severe frost followed by a heavy snowfall. If the deer had survived the radiation, the snow would have made them easy targets for hunters. If the hunters had survived. A strange sight, snow, when the trees are still thick with leaves — some of them turning their bright fall colours, others as green as spring. Stigson and others say the weather has changed and that the seasons have become more erratic. To me it always seems the same, even people's complaints about disastrous long-range weather trends.

In fact, it often seems to me that Stigson's father and his friends have not — as intended — wrought their mighty change upon the world. On the surface, yes: mail, telephones, fuel, cars — most of the amenities of the last hundred years gone. So too, of course, a certain number of people. Lately there has been no news of anywhere aside from the fantastic rumours and stories brought by the occasional wanderer hoping to earn a few nights of meals by bringing us such entertainments. But in the year following the Indian accident, the year in which it and the other "accidents" filled every layer of the earth's atmosphere, every windstream, with clouds of radioactive gases — during that year and especially near the end, you could still watch the nightly television news and see helicopters passing over ruined or deserted cities all over the globe.

Mynor Jones was waiting for me. Or so it seemed as I came out of the woods and found him sitting on the front steps of his house, drinking his terrible whisky and smoking a wild tobacco cigar. The moon was a bright sharp crescent, glistening in the November sky. The sky itself cold and perfectly clear. Like crystal, I thought, and we the butterflies preparing to be frozen.

From the darkness behind him, Mynor Jones pulled a glass. We drank. In the sharp silvery night light his face looked like a rock sledge-hammered into shape.

After a while he led me down to the garden. Half of it was a rubble already eaten or stored, the rest was covered with ragged remnants of canvas, old sheets, even some precious transparent plastic. From beneath one of the plastic covers Mynor Jones pulled two tomatoes. Mine was half-ripe; one side sweeter than summer, the other bitter and hard, tasting of cold sour earth.

"When I was a boy," Mynor Jones said, "my mother squoze the frost out of the ground. Every morning in November she mashed the ground in her fists. You could hear the icicles breaking. And in the spring, just as soon as the snow started to melt, she was out here stomping, kicking, pounding, squeezing the ice into water. She hated snow. At least once every winter she tried to pour kerosene on top and throw a match to the whole thing. Never worked. Too easy. Only way to get rid of the stuff was to smash it to bits. Or wait until summer."

I had met Mynor Jones's mother often enough. A big fat woman, during the tourist season she was to be found perched on a stool at the checkout of the local 5-and-10. From Victoria Day until Labour Day she wore the same blue print dress to work. By mid-July you could smell it as soon as you came into the store. When August was hot, the whole town reeked of it. She used to love to break open rolls of coins. So why not snow? At least on this particular evening I was willing to believe it.

"Your friend doesn't like me," Mynor Jones said.

"Annie?" I asked, knowing better.

Mynor Jones laughed, making the sound of a small rockslide. We were still standing in the garden. The drug was at work again, melting my feet into the ground. I sank to my knees, grabbed handfuls of earth and mashed them into my face. Tiny stones scraped my newly shaven cheeks. Ice too; the temperature was dropping fast, I suddenly realized; under cover of darkness the heat was being sucked from ground and sky to be whisked away to

another part of the planet. I imagined myself
howling in protest, howling like those dying coyo-
tes. I began to laugh. Mynor Jones jumped on top
of me and started trying to bury my head. While we
wrestled, I kept laughing and barking. The plastic
roofing of Mynor Jones's makeshift hothouse was
collapsing on top of us. Jones had his hands
around my throat when I finally found a yellow
elephant squash and brought it down on his head.
A soft plonking sound that made me start laughing
all over again. Mynor Jones backed off and I
slithered away under the canvas, snaking through
prickly squash vines until I got into the higher
terrain of staked peas and green beans. When I
finally came out into the open air on the other side
Mynor Jones was waiting for me, bottle in hand. I
drank and then spat out the terrible whisky along
with a few stray bits of ground that had come to
visit the inside of my mouth. My tongue was
swollen. One molar felt loose.

"Not bad for an old man," Mynor Jones said,
puffing out chest and belly.

"Not bad," I agreed. Then drove my fist as hard
as I could into Mynor Jones's overblown gut. It was
like punching a sandbag. My fist crumpled into
itself and jolts of pain exploded out my elbow.
Mynor Jones laughed.

We crossed the field to a road. Walked along it to
a turning. Climbed the hill to where Mynor Jones's
grandfather had built a smokehouse for venison
and ham. We opened the door. Mynor Jones started
making a fire. A row of pheasants were hanging
upside-down from an oak beam along the back. No
one from the cult knew how to trap birds or game.
Even when Mynor Jones put a handful of meat into

one of her stews, Annie pretended the chunks were
just chewy potatoes. Jones trimmed some fat off one
of the birds, threw it in a frying pan with an onion
and some wild herbs.

"Big belly needs to be fed," Mynor Jones said.
The fat in the pan spluttered. Grease fell into the
fire, sending up blue flares and puffs of smoke.
Soon Mynor Jones was leaning over the pan, using
both hands to shovel food into his bearded face.
The smell was too much to resist: I joined in, we ate
until dawn when, bellies full of charred flesh, we
staggered out of the smokehouse and down the hill
to a stream where we could lie face first to drink,
then to rest our heads in the icy water to let it
thunder through our hair.

I lie beside Annie. This is the third day of snow.
Stigson says that to go inside is a sign of weakness,
a cause of weakness. Staying inside, seeking shelter,
needing to protect the body: these are, Stigson says,
the beginnings of the inevitable decline, the pushing of oneself down the slow hill that can lead only
to an eternity in the bone fields.

Two weeks ago — or was it a month? — Stigson
and I tried to patch it up. Whatever it is that needs
to be patched, which isn't easy to define because we
have never openly quarrelled about anything, just
slowly drifted apart while the others in our group
become listless and confused.

To make it like old times we spent the whole
night walking, the way we used to, first over the
paths forged by our cult, then onto the dirt roads we
used to walk when we were summer visitors. Along
the road we stopped at burnt-out farmhouses and
reminisced about the families that had lived there,
the cars they had driven only a dozen years ago, the
relative beauty of their daughters and the stupidity

of their sons. All dead. From time to time as though such tricks could pull me back into his circle, Stigson would loop his arm around my shoulder to pat me on the back.

At one point Stigson said, "I think this winter is the final test. We're really turning the corner now. In the spring I'm certain we'll blossom again." Listening to him I felt irritated. A year ago he had allowed himself to be baptised by a visiting missionary from a Christian cult that had a farming collective to the north. Since then, like the missionary, he had been talking about "blossoming again" — the new code word for having babies — as though the Chinese revolution were coming.

"No one can stay pregnant, let alone have babies," I replied.

"In the spring," Stigson said. "When we have passed the test."

All of Stigson's recent sermons had centred around the idea that God was testing us, that he had winnowed out the weak, that all of us who remained were strong, ready for the future.

"You and Annie could have a child," Stigson said. We were in a shallow valley, yet even the slight hollow had been enough for me to feel the extra coolness in the air, and before Stigson had spoken I had been poking my feet into the grass at the side of the road to see if the dew was starting to freeze.

Now Annie is sleeping and I am lying beside her. It is not late, I am not tired. But I am in bed with Annie because she wanted to sleep and I wanted to be sure she would be warm. Last winter, too, she went through strange spells of exhaustion, unwillingness to eat, always followed by a revival. So I am trying to convince myself that this is just another episode from which she will recover.

From outside I hear footsteps in the snow. I get

out of bed. I am already dressed, but coming out
from the covers into the crisp air of the room I need
another coat. By the time Stigson comes in I am
sitting in a chair, waiting for him in the dark, boots
tightly laced and an axe in my hand.

"I was worried about you," Stigson says.

"Annie was sick."

"Bringing her inside only makes it worse. Not
right away but the next time."

"If I didn't bring her in, there might not be a next
time."

"Fear is never a wise counsellor," Stigson quotes
from himself. But his heart isn't in it.

We're talking. We're arguing. It's dark but for the
reflected ghostly light of snow. Mynor Jones comes
into the room. Stigson and I can't stop shouting.
Suddenly I am holding the axe in the moonlight.
Annie is screaming. The blade is shining dull
reflected silver. I am, the way Stigson taught me,
outside of myself. I see Stigson approaching me. I
feel my muscles — a flock of birds knowing what to
do, where to go, migrate through the darkness. I see
Stigson falling, one hand outstretched, falling the
way I once taught him, silent as death towards the
unsuspecting prey.

Digging the grave takes two days. Finally we
have to make brush fires to thaw our way through
the frozen crust of ground. By the third day, when I
go back to the "theatre" where the cult used to
gather to sleep or to listen to Stigson's sermons,
everyone has already moved on, drifted away. To
the Christian collective in the north, I suspect, but
they don't need to worry — no one will chase them
down. The fires are out, garbage and unwanted
utensils are neatly stacked in one place. I throw

these remains into the smallest of the caves, then spend the day blocking its mouth with fieldstones. One day, I think, perhaps Stigson will be a great legendary martyr. And I, as he predicted, his Judas. As I walk back to Mynor Jones's house, I am thinking about Stigson, admiring him. Night falls. I am skirting the lake because the ice is not yet thick enough to bear me. If there are other sounds in the forest I cannot hear them for my own, and with each step I grow larger because I am the one who survived.

The Zeidman Effect

The Zeidman Effect

Before his marriage there had been a relationship, an affair, something for which Zeidman had no word. The woman's name was Rachel Strong; she was a second flautist with the London Symphony orchestra. That Zeidman met her at all was a miracle of coincidence because he didn't live in London — in fact had never been there. He was at the time a piano student in Paris, and when his teacher was engaged to give a recital in London he kindly asked Zeidman to accompany him as assistant and baggage-carrier. After the concert there was a reception at which someone said to Zeidman that there was another Canadian musician in the room, which is how he was introduced to Rachel Strong: as a Canadian.

Zeidman was then in his late twenties and had just won third prize in a Warsaw piano competition, a prize which was to entitle him to perform several concerts and had as well given him that first flush of success which allowed him to look at his younger musical colleagues in a suitably paternal way.

"You must be finding it a struggle," he said to Rachel.

"Not really," she said, "my parents have a lot of money."

Zeidman looked away in disgust while reminding himself that one of the reasons he had left Canada was to escape the spoiled rich children who thought of themselves as musicians.

"I miss Canada," Rachel said. "Do you?"

"No."

"You know," Rachel said, "it always surprises me to see what snobs Canadians become the moment they cross the ocean. I suppose you tell everyone in Paris that you're an American in exile, trying to stay out of the army."

The next night they had met at another party, a crowded affair in a house on Hampstead Heath. The year was 1965, loud psychedelic music was blaring from the record players, Rachel was wearing a skirt so short that Zeidman found himself uncomfortably aware of her thighs. But it was, he assured himself, only by chance that he allowed himself to get backed into the same corner as her as midnight came around. Then there was a fight — loud cursing, dishes broken and Zeidman, again the elder compatriot, found himself hustling Rachel out of the house. For a few minutes they stood on the front lawn listening to the music.

"I don't want to go back in," Rachel said.

"I'll see you home."

"I can find my own way, thank you."

"I insist," said Zeidman.

It had been a warm spring day but with the night the temperature had dropped and Zeidman offered his jacket to Rachel. "No, really, I'm all right." But then, as they walked, she linked her arm through his and shivered next to him as the underground train whisked them across the city. At her house there was scotch whisky. After two drinks Rachel turned off the light and said, "I don't want to be alone tonight." An invitation made in such a way as to tell Zeidman that such invitations had been made before. He was about to refuse when Rachel crossed the room and stood next to him for a moment, then put her hands on his face and said, "Please, I really am frightened. You don't have to make love to me, just sleep in my bed."

Even twenty years later, Zeidman, with his eyes closed, could remember the exact words, the exact inflections, the exact sweet feel of her breath on his lips. But as for her face, the colour of her eyes, even details much more intimate — time had stolen them away, leaving only blurred and fuzzy recollections.

"I know that you think of her," his wife would say, "why don't you ever talk about it?"

But Zeidman, truthfully, would shake his head and say that he hardly even remembered her, that he couldn't believe whatever it was or wasn't had taken place. "You're the one I love," Zeidman would say. "She never even crosses my mind." The only times he thought of Rachel were times when she popped into view unexpectedly. Now, for example, as he sat on the airplane reading a magazine article about the tourist delights of Florence — a city they had visited together. But then she was gone and Zeidman found himself looking out the window to see a burst of lights as the wheels of the airplane made contact with the tarmac. After a few unexpected bounces the airplane began to taxi towards the terminal, not without a warning from the captain to keep seat belts fastened and to remain seated until the stewardesses gave the signal to move.

Uncomfortably aware of his blurred reflection in the window, Zeidman turned back to his magazine. He looked longingly at the colour photographs of Florence, he tried to tell himself that but for chance, but for a sudden twist of fate and time, it might have been Florence in which he was arriving, fabulous, beautiful, exotic Florence which was awaiting him with her pale Italian arms flung open, her half-naked madonnas leaping off the walls to whisk him from the airport to the restaurants panting to feed him, the rosy wines uncorking themselves in a frenzy of hospitality. Ah Firenze, yes, but in the meantime fate and time had twisted, both of them, and Zeidman was landing at the newly expanded Halifax airport.

Zeidman, being Zeidman, already knew how it would be. "In fact," he had said to his wife only a few hours ago, "I can already tell you that when I come off the plane a woman will be waiting for me. She will have white hair, dyed blue, and will be wearing an embarrassing print dress that she bought to celebrate her election as president of the local symphony association. No — excuse me — ten years ago she would have been wearing floral prints, but now she is decked out in tasteful mono-colour wool and has a flower in the button of her overcoat. 'Nathan Zeidman,' she barks out. (She has a voice like a lapdog.) 'Over here, please, Professor

Zeidman, Doctor Zeidman, what a wonderful pleasure to have you here. You look just like your
photographs but far more distinguished.'"

"I know," Zeidman's wife sighed sympatheti-
cally. To tell the truth her sighs sounded almost
rehearsed to Zeidman, but then so did his own lines.
The truth was that for the twelve years since his
arrival back in Canada to take up a professorship,
Zeidman's concert career had been reduced to a
gradually diminishing string of performances in
cities which at the time of Beethoven and Mozart
had been either entirely non-existent or, at best, fur-
trading posts populated by porridge-eating remnants of the British Empire.

Before leaving Zeidman went to say good-bye to
his son. The boy was twelve years old, the product,
Zeidman had often bitterly reflected, of seed too
long preserved. He was sitting on the floor of
Zeidman's study and the changing images from the
television set were galloping like wild animals
across his face. Zeidman put his hand on the boy's
shoulder. "I'll be back in two days." The boy
turned to look at him. Zeidman bent towards the
soft white skin of his son's face, pecked at the lips
trustingly offered to his. Then, as he turned back to
the doorway, his son said, "Two days." The voice
was slightly slurred, the way it always would be,
and inside his chest Zeidman felt a familiar little
explosion of humiliation, not unmixed with love.

When he got off the plane, no one was waiting for
him. Zeidman experienced a moment of irritation,
then followed the signs towards the luggage. In the
old days he had travelled differently, always rushing
straight from the airport to the hotel where Rachel

might be awaiting him in bed; in those days he liked to make a game of eluding whomever might have been sent to meet him, Nathan Zeidman, the astonishing pianist who after five years of mediocre performances in festivals had suddenly won prizes in half a dozen competitions and played like a meteorite plunging inspirationally to oblivion.

"Nathan Zeidman," read the cardboard sign. The hands that held it were pale and slim, as was the young woman they belonged to. "Mr Zeidman? Excuse me, I couldn't find a picture. My mother was supposed to pick you up but she was called out of town on business. Sorry, I know she is terribly disappointed to have missed you. If you're still going to be in town tomorrow, she is very anxious to have you for dinner." She tucked the sign under her arm.

"Thank you," Nathan Zeidman said. "Please don't worry about it."

A few minutes later Zeidman had taken his luggage from the conveyor belt and they were in the car, making the long drive from the airport towards the city. It was near midnight and the sun had set hours ago. Yet because of the moon, the sky had a strangely luminous quality and as they drove Zeidman could see the jagged outline of the evergreen trees. He opened the window. A faintly salty smell rushed into the car and Zeidman remembered the first time he had come to Halifax, his drive north from the city where he had seen long, deserted sandy beaches lined with sparse vegetation, all of it growing away from the wind and sea.

"Do you know the city?"

"Not really," Zeidman said. "I was here once or twice before."

"Everyone is very excited that you are coming here. My mother says that all the tickets for your concert have been sold out for two months. Yesterday they played one of your records on the radio. I was very impressed."

There was a burst of multicoloured light. Suddenly they were surrounded by shopping centres and late-night gas stations. And then they were on a toll bridge and Zeidman was searching in his coat pockets for change.

"No, please, I have it here." The pale fingers fumbled in the purse. Finally the correct pieces of silver were extracted and thrown into the waiting basket. Then the hands wrapped themselves around the wheel again and the drive into the city commenced. "We put you at the best hotel," the girl said. "My mother said it was the least we could do." This time Zeidman thought he detected a note of sarcasm in her voice. And why not? What a farce it was that Nathan Zeidman, the prodigy who had collapsed, was now relentlessly touring the provincial capitals of his native land, trying to capitalize on a reputation he had ceased to deserve decades ago. He remembered how he had looked in the dark reflecting glass of the airport as he had carried out his suitcase: a little too wide, abundant white hair like a dyed cap on his head, his suitcase so large it made his arms and legs look as short as dolls' limbs.

"Here we are, Mr Zeidman." Before he could stop her the girl had leapt out of the car and was getting his suitcase from the back seat. While he swung his feet out of the door Zeidman tried desperately to remember her name, so he could thank her properly. To help himself he tried to picture her introducing herself at the airport — which he couldn't

— or himself asking her what her name was. But neither of these two memories was available. Perhaps he had never known — most likely he had just allowed her to call him Mr Zeidman, say "Please, Mr Zeidman," "Excuse me, Mr Zeidman," without even asking himself who she might be.

"I'll check you in, Mr Zeidman," and again she acted before he could protest, marching through the door carrying his valise to the registration desk.

"Are you hungry?" she asked, after Zeidman had signed in.

"I ate on the plane."

"Perhaps you would like to have a drink? Or would you rather be alone." She hesitated. Her face was as narrow and pale as her fingers, almost attractive in its helplessness. Zeidman was on the verge of accepting when she added: "Or perhaps you're tired after your flight. My mother said not to bother you."

"Really," Zeidman said, "you're not bothering me." If he and Rachel had had a daughter, she would have been about this girl's age, perhaps a little older. What a comfort that would have been for his declining years, a daughter to pamper and comfort him.

"My mother told you about the interviews with the newspaper and the radio station tomorrow?"

"Yes," Zeidman said.

"I admire you for refusing to be on television."

"Thank you."

"And tomorrow afternoon there are a few people who would like to meet you for drinks and a light meal before the concert? That is still all right?"

"Of course," Zeidman said. "I am honoured that you have taken so much trouble over me."

"The honour is ours," said the girl. She looked away from him and Zeidman realized that she was very uncomfortable and was waiting for him to say she could leave.

"Thank you very much for picking me up at the airport. I always feel stupid coming in to a strange city in a taxi."

"It was my pleasure, Mr Zeidman, really."

"Good night," Zeidman said. He extended his hand.

"Good night." The girl extended her own hand, which Zeidman felt trembling in his own. Then she turned and left, walking quickly, Zeidman saw, so quickly that she could be seen slowing herself down, for decorum's sake, before waving good-bye to him and disappearing through the revolving door.

"Mr Zeidman, please, excuse me? We met last night."

Zeidman, the sun bright in his eyes, was suddenly aware that the woman he had been staring at as she approached him on the crowded sidewalk had now stopped altogether and was looking at him. She had large sensuous lips to which generous amounts of lipstick had been applied, thick black hair that curled just above her shoulders, green eyes that were flecked like a cat's in the bright light. The light, in fact, was so strong that her skin seemed almost transparent and he could see tiny imperfections struggling towards the surface — perhaps summer freckles which had already begun their long winter hibernation.

"Mr Zeidman, are you all right?"

"Mrs Schonfield, Melanie Schonfield," Zeidman

said, taking the chance of uttering the name that came into his head; but even as he spoke it and she smiled he knew he was right — this woman was the Melanie Schonfield of whom his hostess had spoken, the young pianist and composer who was supposed to be so gifted. "Excuse me, please, for being so slow but the sun was in my eyes and I was thinking about something else."

"Oh, I'm sorry, you seemed to be staring at me as you walked. Of course I didn't realize that the sun was —"

"Please, Mrs Schonfield, don't apologize, it was entirely —"

"Mr Zeidman, I wanted to say how wonderfully you played last night. It had always been my nightmare that something would go wrong like that, at the beginning. I would never have had the courage to recover."

Zeidman felt again the sensations which had gripped him when the notes had suddenly disappeared from his fingers. Terror? No, not exactly. A feeling of calm, in fact, an unexpected serenity. The thought had even crossed his mind that this moment was like a Buddhist enlightenment — a sudden flash of peace and silence splitting apart the tension of normal existence and giving him a sudden sensation of oneness, of fulfillment without effort. But then the oasis had begun to erode and he had become conscious of the nervousness of the spectators, their growing awareness that the silence they were hearing was not part of the music, that in fact he had gone blank and they were teetering together ... But where? On the edge of disaster? Surely not, he had thought — because if 500 people are sitting in a warm and sheltered hall, their bottoms comfortably married to soft cushions, their wool and fur coats snuggled around them — what tragedy would it be if the music stopped? Perhaps they, too, could share his sensations of oneness. Perhaps they, too, could feel flooding into their empty centres the welcome knowledge that beyond their busy and frenetic mental olympics was this restful, peaceful ocean.

And then the music had come back into his hands and he began to play again: but this time it was no — as the *New York Times* critic had once put it — "pyrotechnic cascading waterfall," nor even, as one of Austria's most eminent musicologists had written to him, "a mournful and mystical rendition of our innermost heart played out in the immaculate lyric of Liszt." No, even as he played, Zeidman had felt his efforts for what they were — a forced march taking the place of a wild and abandoned dance. And yet with each measure his confidence returned and even when he asked himself if he knew what was coming in two minutes' — ten minutes' — time, he could visualize the score upon the page, the lines indicating not only the notes to be played by himself but the parts for the orchestra. Then and only then, when his confidence in his ability to complete the concerto was entirely established, did he dare to look from his hands to Donato, the young conductor who had greeted him with such hypocritical reverence. And when he had looked at Donato the younger man had returned his gaze directly, looking straight into his eyes, smiling at him so frankly and so warmly that Zeidman, plodding along with his fingers feeling like frozen little tombstones, couldn't help feeling grateful.

"Really, Mr Zeidman, I did admire your courage

last night. In fact I have always been a fan of yours.
Do you know I have six of your records? Two of
them in copies because I can't bear to listen to them
damaged.''

Zeidman smiled but he felt it was a cruel thing
for her to have said: after all, if a few scratches could
damage a performance, surely a total mental collapse had been even worse. He turned away from
her. He had met her type a hundred times — young
musicians bitter about their own careers, wanting
to test themselves against someone who had done
better.

"I don't mean to take up your time, Mr Zeidman,
you must be rushing to catch your plane."

"No," Zeidman said, "I'm not."

"If you are staying another night, I would very
much like to invite you to have dinner with me."

"Well," Zeidman said, "that is very kind of you."
The truth was that he had decided to stay another
night because after his fiasco he couldn't face his
wife right away. His plan had been to pass the day
wandering the city — it had never occurred to him
that he would be recognized — and then to have
dinner in his room along with a bottle of scotch.
The alcohol would, as it had a few times before,
dissolve everything. He had told his wife that his
stomach was too upset to face an airplane right
away and she had, as always when he said this,
suggested he stay the extra night.

Now Melanie's face flushed a deep scarlet and
Zeidman realized that since her invitation he had
done nothing but let the seconds pass by while he
stood staring at her, lips pursed, mind careening
from pillar to post.

"I'm sorry," he said. "I seem to be falling apart."

His words frightened him so much that he reached out and grasped her arm. "Would you come for a drink with me?" Then he laughed. "I'm sorry, I'm so helpless, I don't even know if bars are open this time of day."

As it turned out they weren't, but there was a liquor store near the hotel which Melanie led him to; then they took the bottle up to Zeidman's room.

"We could go to my place," Melanie offered twice, but Zeidman didn't want to.

"No please, I couldn't be in a house right now. What I need is an anonymous room, a hotel. Please understand, I have no wicked intentions."

Zeidman had tried to take a nap after lunch so when they entered the room he felt briefly embarrassed at the sight of the imperfectly made bed, the naked pillow on top of the covers with the impression of his head still visible, like a footprint in a Hollywood sidewalk. But beyond the bed — a gigantic king-size conglomeration of mattresses and covers that made Zeidman even more self-conscious than usual about his diminutive size — there were two comfortable armchairs.

"You sit down," Melanie said. "I'll get the drinks."

Zeidman obeyed. A week ago had been his fifty-second birthday and in his photographs, the ones Melanie had seen, he looked well-preserved and vigorous — a man so firmly ensconced in the prime of life that when he was asked for autographed portraits of himself he signed his name with a flourish that covered half the picture, European style. He watched Melanie as she settled in. Between them, on the coffee table, was a bottle of scotch, two empty glasses plus one full of ice cubes, an ashtray.

Zeidman felt as though he was about to celebrate his own wake.

After two drinks Zeidman began to talk. What came out of his mouth was no surprise but he had never said it before. He talked about how he had gone to Europe in his early twenties, hoping that study at the Paris Conservatoire would somehow propel him into the company of concert pianists. He explained to Melanie, as though she didn't know, that in the whole world there were only fifty good concert careers at any one time and that fighting for those fifty slots in the public eye were literally thousands of highly trained, highly ambitious, pianists. "Partly it is a matter of attrition," Zeidman said. "Not everyone can take the uncertainty. My piano teacher told me that by the time I was thirty there would be only 500 left. Half of those would be women — but women get married, he said. By the time I was thirty-five there would only be 300. And by the time I was forty, if I hadn't made it, it would be too late."

He looked to see what Melanie would say, but Melanie only listened. She had taken her shoes off, her feet were on the table. She wasn't wearing stockings so Zeidman could see her naked toes. On the nails was bright red polish, which matched her lipstick.

"I was almost thirty when I made my first placing: a third prize in Warsaw. I was still studying with the same teacher. Then I fell in love. It was a disaster, of course, but very romantic. I started to place second in the competitions, then first. Two years after Warsaw I was the only slightly elderly wunderkind of Europe. I played seventy-five concerts that year. Seventy-five! Even in my dreams I had only hoped for fifty. The next year I played a hundred. There were records, television appearances, debuts in one capital after another. For a while I saved all the reviews in a special pocket of my suitcase. Rachel, meeting me, always had new ones to add. And then finally there were too many to bother and one night, drunk on champagne, we shredded them into confetti.''

Zeidman's eyes were closed. The confetti incident was one he had told to his wife. In that story there had been a bottle of champagne and the two of them had danced about the hotel room, celebrating his ascendancy to Olympus. What he had omitted was that the reviews had been torn up not in ecstasy but in anger. It had happened in a hotel room in Rome, after what at that time had been one of his usual dazzling triumphs, an evening when sitting at the piano he had felt a quicksilver sureness with every note and the music had seemed not so much to come from him as through him, so bent over the piano he had merely closed his eyes and abandoned mind and body to whatever fate held in store. At the end, while the audience wildly applauded, Zeidman, too, had wanted to applaud — not himself but the gods who had allowed him to be a vehicle for their passion.

After the recital they had gone back to the hotel and Zeidman, in the bathroom shaving, had curiously opened Rachel's purse to see what new journalistic extravaganzas she had found for him since their last meeting. But picking out a sheet of paper he found himself reading not praise for his lightning little fingers but praise for the bodily gifts of his beloved. The offending piece of paper was in fact a letter from another lover, a letter which described in detail the intimate charms of which time had now robbed him.

"What is this?" Zeidman had demanded, carrying the letter extended in his fingers like a filthy piece of laundry. "What is this piece of garbage doing in your purse?" Without being able to help himself he had turned beet red and begun to tremble. "What are you trying to do, ruin me?"

"Ruin you," Rachel had shouted back at him, not humbled but suddenly ferocious. "Ruin you! What a joke. I haven't ruined you, I've made you." Then she stepped up to him, livid, and snatched the letter out of Zeidman's hand.

"What is this?" Zeidman roared. "Is this some kind of joke? Is that what this is?"

"This is greatness," Rachel had screamed. "Passion, tragedy, romance. Admit it, you've known all along I would never be faithful to you. What do you think I am, one of your ridiculous lower-class Canadian hausfraus? If you want me so much stop whining about it and take me. Take me, you coward, take, take, take!"

"You're already taken!" Zeidman howled back at her. He had first ripped up her letter and then, in a frenzy of anger, the reviews she had saved for him in her purse followed by all the reviews in his special suitcase pocket.

"What did she want me to do?" Zeidman now asked Melanie. "Was I supposed to tear her to pieces like a wild animal? Maybe I should have."

But Melanie said nothing, only re-filled the glasses and looked at Zeidman with a sad smile on her lips. The bottle of scotch was almost gone. So was the daylight. Now the room was plunged into a strange scarlet twilight made by the setting sun as it

filtered through the red curtains. Zeidman took a
sip from his new drink, then began talking again:
this time he told Melanie how he had known that
night his relationship — a romance, a comedy, a
thing for which he had no word — with Rachel was
over. But still, it lingered on for two more years
until he met an Englishwoman one day in France,
at a party at the Canadian Embassy. The Englishwoman had pursued him, he didn't know why, but
it turned out she was sexy and comfortable. After a
while he knew he would never find a letter in her
purse and that was when he decided to marry her
and go back to Canada.

"Did you love her?"

"Of course," Zeidman said. "I still love her. And I
have always been faithful to her." He stood up and
turned on a light.

"Do you mind if I smoke?" Melanie asked.

"Please, go ahead. In fact, may I have one?
Sometimes I smoke when I am very tired."

Zeidman went out to the hall to get more ice
cubes. When he came back into the room, Melanie
was slumped back in her armchair, smoking, but
now beside the bottle of scotch was a package of
cigarettes.

Zeidman turned off the light again, then lay
down on the bed. "You don't mind?" he asked. "I
really am very tired."

"Would you like me to leave?"

"Oh no, please, I want you to stay."

Zeidman lay on his back and watched the red tip
of Melanie's cigarette as it made the trip back and
forth between the ashtray and her mouth.

"It took a long time to arrange things in Canada.
I wanted to return as a professor. Meanwhile I still

had concerts to play, records to make. But something had gone out of it. I felt as though my talent was a pearl that Rachel had uncovered but now I was growing an increasingly complicated shell to protect it; until finally, one day I discovered that the pearl had been eaten by the shell and only the shell was left."

Zeidman sighed. Finally he had done it; he had told the story of himself as a failure. For twenty years he had been saving it up and now he had finally said it.

"What bullshit," Melanie said.

"Life is terrible," agreed Zeidman.

"No, not life, you." Then she came and sat down beside him on the bed. The first thing she did was to take off his shoes. Then his socks. When she began kissing his feet they felt very far away to Zeidman, which told him that he was very drunk. Then she unbuttoned his shirt, undid his belt. Zeidman began to feel less drunk. When she kissed him, her lips were soft and smoky, like oysters. Then Zeidman made love to her. During it he thought that this love-making was warm, was like being in the magical South Seas where the animals invented themselves before crawling ashore. No crashing symphony of waves but, nonetheless, a lovely little sonata full of counterpoints and rills.

"Not bad," Melanie said when it was finished. "Pretty good for a failure."

"Not bad," Zeidman agreed. The room was warm, he was lying naked on his back, sweat still pleasantly moist on his chest and thighs. He lit a cigarette. He was fifty-two years old. He watched the tips of their cigarettes dancing like fireflies in the darkness. Just like in a movie. And, just like in a movie, he knew exactly what would happen. It would come back to him now, the music, and his next few concerts would go well. Sometimes Melanie would come to meet him in strange cities, perhaps he would even find a way of dedicating his new career to her.

"Zeidman does his best work in twenty years," the reviews would say. This time he would save them. Then Melanie would find someone else or, if she took too long, he would. Life would go on. His son would offer him his lips to be kissed. The next silence would be the last.

Mirrors

Mirrors

I

He couldn't help the little symptoms — heart thumping, palms sweating, images sliding out from beneath each other like cards tumbling from a deck. Paranoia, Carolyn called it, with a certain gentle smile that was supposed to soften the word. And so, when he saw the house lights were on, his first feeling was relief.

Then — because it was spring, he would say to himself later, and there was no foliage — his headlights picked out Michael's truck parked at the bottom of the driveway. That would be for her suitcases — his heart accelerated again — and even as he turned from the road into the driveway, cutting motor and lights, he couldn't help anticipating the sight of those suitcases, lined up in a hostile row. Drifting down between the maples he waited until the last moment, only a few feet from the truck, to put on the brakes. Even so, coasting slowly, his wheels slipped on the ice and his car jolted into the truck hard enough to slam his head forward into the steering-wheel.

Outside, Jonathan found himself sucking at the cool air as if air alone could save him. Then, as his head cleared, he became aware of the river's sound; a roar that grew louder, more intense, more layered with backwashes, swirls, chunks of grinding ice as he walked towards it. Until finally, lying face down on the bank of the wide river, the trembling earth and rushing water were almost enough to break him open and carry him away —. Almost.

As he was walking back to the house, every breeze seemed heavy with the smells of stirring mud, budding trees, the melting rot of frozen vegetation that had been covered by snow for six months. Easy to imagine the waiting armies of summer, billions of spores sheltered in the earth, lying between grains of soil and preparing to explode.

For a moment Jonathan stayed in the driveway, lighting a cigarette. He was standing beside the stone firepit they used for boiling maple sap down to syrup, but tonight there was no sign that only a week ago the three of them had been by the fire — the best of friends — passing wine and cigarettes from hand to hand.

Jonathan began walking towards the house. Either they had heard him or they had not. The kitchen lights were on; as he stepped in he could see no signs of packing, only the remains of supper on the table. Also a half bottle of wine. Interesting, he found himself noting, it had been years since a bottle of wine had gone unemptied on his table. From the living-room there were no sounds of conversation or music. Jonathan wondered what it would be like to go in and see his wife and his best friend going at it on the carpet. Or maybe they preferred the couch. A choice: before it was too late he could turn around, walk out, get back into his car and drive to a hotel in Kingston. He tried to imagine himself at the wheel of his car again. His belly was churning. He went to the cupboard and took out a bottle of scotch. Found a clean glass, poured himself two fingers and drank it down. Holding the glass he noticed that something unexpected had happened to the tips of his fingers: they were vibrating, on their own, like frog's legs detached from the body. Then he heard footsteps from the living room. They had been in there, after all. A voice talking in normal tones. No moans of sex, no intimate undercurrents, no trace in Carolyn's voice of anything he didn't hear every day. In a few seconds she would be in the kitchen. Glad to see him, no doubt, at least on the surface. Anxious to reassure him that despite everything he had threatened, she was still the faithful and enduring wife. No doubt she would joke at his expense about the stupid trick he had tried to play, coming home two days early from the conference, unannounced, spying like a primitive ape.

The steps had temporarily paused. She would be, Jonathan knew, beside the thermostat. Whenever she stopped at the thermostat it meant she was cold, that she wanted to turn up the heat. And then Carolyn was in the kitchen. They were standing there — Jonathan thought, unable to do anything but think — looking at each other. He was holding the bottle of scotch. She was naked. What she might have been thinking was unknown to Jonathan; her face was so frozen that he started to laugh.

"Please," Carolyn said. Her arms had been folded

across her chest but now, as her face unfroze and she began to cry, she opened them wide.

Then he was back in the car, driving towards Kingston. Driving fast. His window was open; the cold air was to keep him from going crazy; and he was shouting into the wind — "Bitch! bitch! bitch!" He had left the bitch with her arms spread wide. Tits not what they used to be, to tell the truth, or maybe the harsh kitchen light had failed to flatter. Going up a hill towards town he saw a transport come over the crest. He switched lanes. The transport's high beams flicked at him, then its horn began to blare. Jonathan swerved back into his own lane, pushing the accelerator to the floor. At the top of the hill he paused to make sure the truck was continuing. Then he lit a cigarette, took a drink from the bottle of scotch which had somehow travelled with him from his kitchen, turned his car around and started driving home. It was all so simple, so inevitable, but as he coasted down the driveway — this time lights on, motor running, blood clamouring for blood, he was shouting again. "Bitch! bitch! bitch!"

II

The road was uphill from the house, a massive stone relic set on a grassy plateau overlooking the water. Connecting road and house was a narrow dirt driveway bracketed by rows of giant maples.

When spring came the sunlight blazed down from the sky and was magnified by the snow. Under its force the old maples leaked sap from broken limbs and lightning wounds. Jonathan identified with these trees, describing to me the way his own heart was mending and bleeding under the hot sun of his new love. "Can you believe it?" he would ask, giving me a sweet vulnerable smile I had never seen before, "the old man is stabbed to the very innards, *bleeding* for his love." By the time he had abandoned such metaphors the leaves had already popped out of their buds: lime-green baby leaves so dazzlingly new that when the sun hit them, they turned the sky around them the colour of breaking glass.

"Carolyn bought me this hat," Jonathan said one day. We were standing in the rain under the trees. The leaves had turned brighter yet in the rain and were exploding life into the luminous grey light of the spring afternoon. Sheltering Jonathan from all this action was his new hat, a feather in its band. I thought: how like Jonathan to decorate his new hat with the feather of a dead bird.

Summer twilight. Birds swoop, weaving paths in the cool currents that run with the river. We are on the lawn, our chairs facing the crumpled glassy surface of the moving water. Jonathan is wearing another of Carolyn's gifts, this time a Mexican shirt with a hand-embroidered scoop neck. Around his thick tanned throat is a chain featuring a hammered silver bird, an Incan relic that he discovered on his latest dive into the past.

"Has anyone told you lately that you are a very attractive man?"

Jonathan laughs. I am looking down to the riverbank at a rabbit moving fearfully across the grass.

"You," Carolyn says, "I mean you." Now she is kneeling in front of me, her hands on my knees, her

eyes looking into mine. She has broad cheekbones,
a narrow sculpted nose created by a Toronto surgeon after she took a swan dive, face-first, racing
downhill on a bicycle. Today she is wearing her
own matching Mexican blouse. I am looking at her
and because I have just seen the album of their
journey I am reminded of Carolyn in the pictures,
Carolyn in fact very beautiful, smiling her big
smile, somehow in the foreground of every shot —
as if to say that while the others were tourists and
suckers she was just going along for the screen test.
"What's wrong? You don't have a problem, do
you?" She laughs again and this time I laugh with
her because this is the line Carolyn fed to a weekend
guest I brought to their place — a guest who
retreated from the winter regimen of cross-country
skiing and snowshoeing to get unforgivably drunk
before dinner.

But Carolyn isn't finished yet. She's still kneeling
in front of me, still carrying on with her soprano
laugh. Carolyn and I look at each other. We have
the usual feelings, I have always thought. I am
Jonathan's best friend, so she tolerates me. She
makes Jonathan happy, so I tolerate her. Of course
there's a frosty edge, because Jonathan has told us
each things about the other that are less than
flattering.

Carolyn says, "Well, you know, I'm serious. It's
time you got over your wife and got involved with
someone else." Pause for dramatic effect. "For
longer than a weekend, I mean."

"Don't tease Michael. You know he's the original
Saturday-Night man."

"That's me." I stand up and start walking towards the river. What am I supposed to say?

Unable to sleep I listen through the open window for a breeze. Instead: still air, a porcupine crunching noisily through the brush, moths beating against the screen as they fight their way towards the dial of the illuminated clock.

Two fifty-six.

Across the hall Carolyn and Jonathan are in their bed. Jonathan, like me, so drunk that at midnight we were scarcely able to make our usual trek along the river path.

"Better not drive," Jonathan had said.

"The truck knows its way."

"And miles to go before I sleep. Get a horse."

Sliding into the cool linen. Waiting for sleep. Transported into a weird drunken doze, my mind a crippled butterfly struggling in the dark. Then waking up, half-sober, soaked in sweat. Pushing down the sheet. Hearing the porcupine, the moths. No human breathing. The night gripping tighter.

Two fifty-seven.

I put on my jeans and go downstairs in search of cooler air.

Soon I am in the living-room, settled into one of the comfortable padded chairs in which I have spent dozens of winter evenings emptying the bottle with Jonathan. Until Carolyn came. "But we must forge on," Jonathan would insist, more than keeping pace with me. "Do you know why we have to drink? Drink is to the middle-aged what sleep is to babies. Oblivion, sweet and otherwise. A quick trip to the Barbados. Getting sick and hung over is all part of the voyage. Proves you've been somewhere."

Sitting in the dark, bare skin scratching against the upholstery, toes vacationing on a coffee table, I ask myself where I have been tonight. The Barbados? Not exactly. Escaping something? But what? Maybe I have only been drinking away an otherwise beautiful summer's night. Maybe I have only been sailing a much-crossed sea, wasting moonlight, Jonathan — as always — at the helm, me — as always — riding steerage.

With my toes I try to find a package of cigarettes. Then, perfectly timed, a match scraping, a flare in the darkness, a tear-shaped circle of light. Carolyn.

"Sorry. I didn't mean to frighten you."

"I couldn't sleep. Must have had too much to drink."

Carolyn laughs. "No one keeps up with Uncle Jonathan." She stands up, crosses the room, the glowing tip of her cigarette a monster firefly floating through the darkness. "I took yours. You want one?"

"Thanks."

Her hand brushes mine. "God, it's dark." She puts the cigarette in my lips, then holds her own to light it. "You going?"

She settles down at my feet, leans into my leg. It occurs to me that we have seldom touched: a ritual handshake the first time we met, a compulsory kiss New Year's Eve.

She is wearing a white shift. I am wondering if I will reach down to touch it. Then I draw away, settle into the routine of smoking, breathing, navigating the clouds of tension that are beginning to gather around us.

She turns. She puts her hand on my belly. Slides down to the top button of my jeans.

"No."

"Please?"

Later, sticky with each other, we walk on the lawn holding hands. Then we lie down again, this time in the grass far from the house. I write my name on her neck with my tongue, other tricks I haven't had a chance to try for a long time. After a while I become aware that I am making a strange noise in my throat, the contented baby-like humming my daughter used to make when she was nursing. Carolyn, too, is making noises, little moaning melodies that match my own.

We are lying on our backs. This time we have gotten our clothes off. A late-night sliver of the moon has risen to slice through the darkness.

Jonathan was an expert in old pottery, the kind that comes in shards. A professor of archaeology to be exact. Not only had he travelled to Mexico, but to sites all around the world. Relics, souvenirs, framed pictures of curiosities were scattered through his house. Also in the house, not entirely invisible, were his poems. Poetry was not his profession, which was teaching and research; not his hobby, which was renovating and repairing the home he had owned for more than twenty years; not his love, which was Carolyn and her predecessors. It was merely something he did, among other things, the mark of a civilized man, an adornment like his Mexican shirt, a relative neither close nor distant, who was tolerated, despised and admired. Also, among his many accomplishments, it was the one

about which he was vain. Never would Jonathan
sink to boasting about his latest honour, to meditat-
ing drunkenly on the possibility of another step up
the academic ladder, to leaving open on a table —
as if by chance — this or that scholarly article. But
with his poetry — well — for example: if the bottle
had grown empty and a second was at hand; when
sleepy drunkenness indicated that the narrow end
of the journey was rapidly approaching — then
Jonathan might seize a scrap of paper hitherto
unnoticed, or even pick up the copy of his book
that always seemed to be nearby — and suddenly he
was reading to you in a voice amazingly polished, a
voice smoothly manoeuvring from one word to the
next, a voice rising and falling with the accents of
Literature: in brief, the voice not of Jonathan the
man whom I knew, but of Jonathan the precocious
seminary-boy-turned-successful-scholar — the
voice of the shadow Jonathan, the man-of-the-mind
Jonathan who should have surrounded himself
with a library and spent his nights reading by
candlelight.

When did Jonathan compose his poetry? Travelling from one conference to another, in hotels,
invariably while looking at his own face in the
mirror.

He offered this unexpected revelation in the
tavern where before Carolyn's arrival we had often
passed winter Saturday afternoons. I wondered
what he saw when he looked at himself. What I saw
was a face tanned dozens of times in the tropics, an
amazingly gentle face with rounded features, high
cheekbones to which sun and alcohol had given a
permanent flush of well-being, a broad lined forehead overhung by a thatch of salt-and-pepper hair,
a smile stranded between sly and shy.

"I don't suppose you knew I was so vain about

my looks," Jonathan added after his confession
about the mirror. *Lonely*, I would have said, but
didn't because Jonathan with his sad honest eyes
and his sighs as he settled his weight into a chair
had become — thanks to Carolyn — one of those
people with whom you make certain to communi-
cate every pretence of complete — even careless —
honesty, while in fact taking every precaution to
avoid the truth.

So I said: "In your case, vanity is hopeless," or
something like that — the sort of remark men
expect from each other.

Jonathan said, "It's strange being here in the
summer. I've never been here in the summer
before."

Between us, on the table, was a pitcher of beer.
The tavern was air-conditioned but the pitcher was
sweating small streams of water onto the plastic-
topped table. Jonathan filled our glasses.

"I suppose you're my best friend," Jonathan said.
"That makes it hard. One should probably discuss
these things with strangers."

For a moment I tried to pretend to myself that he
was still talking about his poems. I lit a cigarette,
using it as an excuse to turn my eyes away from
him.

"Carolyn told me everything. At least I think it
was everything. I suppose you never know."

"What did she tell you?"

"About your screwing," Jonathan said. "What
did you think?"

I nodded.

"I'm serious. What did you think she might have
told me?"

"I don't know. I was just hoping she hadn't told
you that."

"Is there anything else?"

I shrugged. "No." *What else is there?* I had thought of adding, just as a diversion. Because there was something else: the talk of love, the continually made and then discarded plans to run away, the little tiffs and reconciliations, spates of jealousy, three secret dinners in town, the one all-night tryst we'd managed to arrange when Jonathan was away, my own recent declaration that I couldn't keep sleeping with her, her response that she was relieved and that the whole thing had been just "physical, cabin fever."

"The three of us could do it together," Jonathan said. "I'm not the jealous type. What do you say?"

"It was my fault. It's all over now. Carolyn loves you very much, Jonathan; you know you mean everything to her."

Jonathan sipped at his beer. "You two should go away for a while, think things over."

I was about to say something back but then I saw that Jonathan's hands were beginning to shake. Strong hands. Hands I now wished would bunch up into fists and send me into at least temporary oblivion.

"We could go out to the parking lot," I offered.

And then suddenly we were out in the drizzling rain, standing between my pickup truck and Jonathan's Chevrolet with its sheepskin-covered seats. We were wavering back and forth, our feet digging into position, me waiting for Jonathan to make a move.

Jonathan put his hand on my shoulder. "She asked me to marry her. She said she needed me."

"She does."

"I think she does," Jonathan said. "That's the crazy thing." Then he made a mock fist and hit me

on the chest, one of those little love-taps men give
to each other except that at the last second Jonathan
closed his fist and swung his whole bulk into the
punch, sending me down into the mud. I was still
sitting there when Jonathan walked away, climbed
into his car, drove off.

"Good luck, you asshole," I shouted as Jonathan
mothered his car over the curb onto the street. And
slapping the mud from my jeans, feeling happy but
also sorry for myself at the same time, I couldn't
help remembering all the times that Jonathan and I
had driven home from this same tavern, zooming
along on foaming rivers of beer, Jonathan singing
out bawdy songs in his full baritone voice while
every few seconds his eyes flicked to the rearview
mirror, watching for ghosts.

III

Carolyn sometimes thought about writing a little
treatise on her life and loves, *Memoirs Of A Timid
Woman* or something like that. Something to be
found in a desk drawer. Something that could
begin: *Like most faculty wives* ... Then she would
go on to explain how she had gone to the party —
but not officially — with her thesis adviser who was
married. That had been something different — a
chance romance — not really a romance but a
perfect flirtation because she had wanted sex and
safety in the same package. *Sex and safety in the
same package.* For that, further explanations would
be required. A quick trip through childhood, the
twentieth century, the Third World War of the
Sexes — *you've seen the movies.*

In this movie the girl was a reluctant mistress

who had heard too many stories about liberated Amazons crashing through the night. But it was the man who cracked first, threatened to fall in love, tell all to his wife and force Carolyn to run away with him. On the way to the party he had told her that "everything" was arranged. He was going to spend a sabbatical year in England studying "the early Wittgenstein." Carolyn, imagining herself wearing damp woollen long-johns while her adviser chased her through an unheated apartment, was unable to speak. Instead, looking for an unforgivable exit, she asked Jonathan if he could drop her at her house.

A few days later Jonathan telephoned and invited her to join him at a restaurant for dinner. All very chaste. And very quickly it was established that they were both single and eligible. "You're *really* not married?" she asked. "Not living with anyone? Not bound to a secret alliance?"

"Just my pottery," Jonathan said. "And my house. In fact, you should come out and see my shards, as they say."

Then she would tell about the drive to his house, a warm comfortable journey bathed in easy conversation and cigarette smoke. Once there, Jonathan made a fire, showed her his collection, told witty anecdotes about his journeys into the past. In return she offered the slim tale of her thesis supervisor and how she had behaved so stupidly she was afraid she would fail her course and lose her scholarship.

"A scholarship student in philosophy!" Jonathan had exclaimed. "Don't worry, they would never take a scholarship away from someone like you."

"Don't tease me."

"I'm not," Jonathan said. "I'm on the committee."

After that there was another drink and then Jonathan said it was time he drove her home, before he became a menace.

"I wouldn't mind staying," Carolyn said. This would look bad in the book, even when she explained that she wanted to stay not because he was on the committee but because he didn't seem to need anything from her.

"I never sleep with students."

"Oh no, I didn't mean *that*. I just meant you could give me the couch, nice and cosy here by the fire, and in the morning you could drop me off at my place on your way to the university."

"Spoken like a true lady."

The visits became regular: once or twice a week, dinner and drinking and conversation. And by midnight she was always alone in her sleeping bag. Buzzing slightly from the liquor, sleepy but not exhausted, she would think about how perfect these evenings were, how sensual rather than sexy, how pleasant it was to fall asleep like an overheated cat in front of the fire.

A couple of months into this routine, the story would continue, Michael appeared on the scene with one of his "weekend visitors." At midnight, before anyone yawned, Carolyn said, "I'll go upstairs now." Which she did, to Jonathan's room. When he came to bed two hours later, she was still awake, sitting cross-legged on his quilt and reading.

He was in a state she had come to recognize: drunk but still navigating. She closed the door behind him, then switched off the light. Without comment Jonathan undressed and slid into bed. Carolyn followed.

"You can go back to the living-room if you want," Jonathan said. "Michael takes his girlfriends to the attic. I think he must have a stash of candles and incense up there." He was lying immobile in his place, not touching her. Carolyn reached out and put her fingers on his ribs. Rough skin, unexpected muscle, a thin layer of sweat.

She began to stroke him very slowly, very carefully, running her hand up and down his side, then across the locked muscles of his wide chest.

"I'm not very good at this," Jonathan finally said. He was still lying rigid, his hands laced behind his head.

"Do me a favour? Don't worry about the details. Can I lie on top of you? I'm freezing."

"Let me be the missionary, I'll lie on top of you."

With these words, *I'll lie on top of you*, Carolyn had always thought the first chapter could end. Or perhaps they were so conclusive in every respect that the second chapter should be a blank, a little opportunity for shared speculation.

Spring and the maples are leaking again, this time into buckets. At the end of the driveway a stone-lined pit. Inside the fire crackles, boiling away the maple sap.

During the day Carolyn tends the fire. She wears a lumberjack shirt Jonathan gave her their first spring. Since then it has been washed and re-washed until the soft cotton surrounds her like a security blanket. Secure, too, is how she feels crouched by the spitting flames, breathing sweet wood smoke and watching the woodpeckers forage through the old maples.

After work, Michael and Jonathan take over. Splitting wood by the light of the flames. Drawing stumps of cedar closer to the fire, clapping hands for warmth and passing a bottle back and forth. When the moon rises it turns the fields into white glowing sheets. The two men walk down to the river, listen to the boom of the ice cracking under the surging pressure of the spring currents.

It's close to midnight before they go into the house. Michael and Jonathan strip off their coats, their thick sweaters. Outside the fire is down to a bed of glowing embers. Beside it, a cord of wood is cut and stacked, waiting to be fed into tomorrow's flames. They eat. They drink red wine. Michael reaches into his briefcase to show the latest picture of his daughter. After all these years the divorce has finally gone through. Michael's ex-wife has moved to Vancouver taking the girl with her — courtesy of the court.

"So," Carolyn says, "you're a free man now."

"That's it," Michael replies.

She watches him as he bends over the soup. His face is narrow, his mouth thin. She is not exactly certain what it was about him that made her want him so much.

As always, Carolyn is the first to go upstairs. At the landing she pauses. The men's voices, engaged in perfunctory conversation during dinner, have now relaxed into lower, slower tones. Jonathan laughs — a mumble of agreeable bass notes. Michael's laugh starts later, ends earlier — higher-pitched, sharper, chipping away at the edges of things.

In her bedroom she undresses, puts on the terrycloth robe Jonathan gave her against the winter cold. There was a period when they went to a marriage counsellor, driving all the way to Toronto so no one could possibly find out, going not because Jonathan was unhappy but because what she wanted against the cold wasn't something you could buy in a store but Jonathan himself, his big bear's body keeping out the demons.

On her bedside table there are books, including Jonathan's poetry. Their first winter Jonathan had written new poems, poems about her body, poems he called love poems. In those honeymoon weeks she would lie against him, listening with her ear at his chest as he declaimed verses in praise of her various parts. Sometimes she would giggle as he compared her breasts to Etruscan vases, or her belly to the vast rolling stretches of the Sahara Desert. "But I'm serious," Jonathan would insist, and then he would slide his hand into her robe and she would giggle some more and accuse him of using verse to incite indecent acts.

Carolyn moves across the room. The fire is still burning, a red heart bleeding slowly into the darkness. She is standing in front of the window. She sees her reflection: a slender face, white teeth when she smiles, long hair curling down to her shoulders. "My Sad Madonna loves to kiss" had been the first line of one of Jonathan's poems; and now he was talking about a whole new book, one that would be dedicated to their life together, to her. Carolyn looks at herself in the mirror and then, thinking about Jonathan's poetry, remembers what Michael told her. She imagines Jonathan sitting in front of a mirror in a Chicago hotel room.

Through the window comes the sound of wind, of men's voices, of a truck door slamming. Carolyn sees the lights go on, hears the familiar uncertain cough of the motor before it catches, watches the twin red tail-lights of Michael's truck as it slowly climbs the driveway towards the road.

She sits cross-legged on the quilt, opens a magazine, begins brushing out her hair. It is Saturday night. Even as she pulls the covers over her she can hear Jonathan's deliberate half-soused step as he climbs towards her. She closes her eyes. He is breathing deeply; there is a pause while he first remembers the new bathroom he has installed, *en suite*, then decides it would be more discreet to use the old one.

Water runs. Carolyn hears the rambunctious sounds of Jonathan splashing his face to sober up. Through the slightly open window she can smell the last traces of the fire.

Jonathan is in the room. Heavily, he climbs into bed, spreads himself immobile beside her, breathes. Some nights, lying like this, listening to him drift slowly into sleep, Carolyn has allowed her mind to wander down certain illegal trails. One that used to be popular: that in another universe she led a twin existence, one where she spent every night with Michael, not Jonathan; betrayed Michael, not Jonathan; made love with Jonathan, not Michael. Another: that she had left Jonathan and was lying in her own bed, alone in a city with no name, and that the only breathing she had to listen to was her own. A third and now the most frequent but most dreaded: that one of these days or nights Jonathan, having drunk, smoked and eaten too much for the three decades of his adult life, was going to have a heart attack. Then she would telephone the ambulance, go with him to the hospital. There he would lie again, on his back, barrel chest and belly covered by a white sheet, oxygen mask over his wide generous mouth, eyes staring hurt and frightened at the ceiling. "There's no hope," the doctor would mouth at her, out of Jonathan's sight. Soon Michael would come to join the vigil and they would stand one on each side of Jonathan's bed, waiting for him to expire.

"I wouldn't want to be left alone with Michael," Carolyn thinks.

"What?" Jonathan shouts. He jerks up in bed. Carolyn, terrified, cringes away from him.

"What's going on? I just want to know what's going on here," Jonathan's voice cries out angrily.

Jonathan's eyes are closed but he has raised his head and is staring through closed eyelids at the ceiling.

"Tell me!" His fist crashes down on the bed. Then he is shaking his head and shoulders, slapping his cheeks gently with his palms. "I'm sorry, did I frighten you? I was having one of those dreams again. Can you get me a cigarette?"

"Do you want me to light it for you?"

"Thanks."

She puts the cigarette between his lips and then, as though it were a caress, slides her hand along his chest to feel his heart. It is beating away, strong and regular as always.

"Night terrors," Jonathan says calmly. "Maybe I should stop drinking."

"You always drink."

"Catches up with you, I guess. At least, it's catching up with me." He switches on the light. "You know what I was dreaming? That you were having an affair with Michael again. That you'd been having it on with him the whole time. God, I was ready to kill the little bastard.''

"And me? Were you going to kill me too?''

"Oh no, I couldn't kill you, even in a dream. I was just going to pack your suitcases and leave them in the snow." Jonathan laughs and Carolyn laughs with him. "As a matter of fact," Jonathan continues, "I'm not feeling very well. Would you mind going down to the kitchen and getting me a scotch-and-water? There's a bottle in the cupboard above the freezer.''

"I was dreaming too — that you were sick. Don't be sick, please." She drops to her knees beside the bed. "Do you want me to call the doctor, Jonathan?''

While in the kitchen Carolyn convinces herself that there is something wrong with him, that it was unlucky for her to dream he was sick while he was having his own nightmares, that the colour of his skin wasn't right, that when she gets back to the room he will be dead. But when she returns Jonathan is sitting quietly in bed, wearing his favourite shaggy pullover and smoking another cigarette.

"Feeling better?''

"All better." He takes the drink, sips at it. "Now I have something to tell you, Carolyn. Go to the window. Look outside. I don't want you to look at me.''

"Please —''

"Do as I say.''

She turns and walks to the window. The fire has gone out. Nothing outside but the pale snow, the faintly seen shadows of leafless maples, the oblong light cast out from their own room.

"I don't want you any more," Jonathan says. "I'm sick of this thing with you and Michael. The secret phone calls, the visits to his apartment when I'm away. The thing is, Carolyn, I used not to mind but now I do. So that's it. It's over. I don't want you any more. Don't worry about your suitcases in the snow. You can stay here for a while, so long as you don't bother me."

"So long as I don't bother you?"

"That's right. Now you can turn around."

"Thank you."

"Perhaps you'd be more comfortable in the living-room."

Carolyn folds her arms over her chest, forces herself to inch across the space between them. Halfway she stops. "No thanks, Jonathan, I'll stay here. This is my bedroom, too." She starts walking again, until finally she is sitting beside him.

Jonathan is holding his glass of scotch. An hour ago he was drunk, stumbling up the stairs. A few minutes ago he had appeared to be dying. Now, looking at him, Carolyn sees a man totally in possession of himself. The way, in fact, he had seemed when she met him: huge, detached, ever more sober the more he drank; a man who needed nothing but the stone house he'd surrounded himself with, and the few friends and acolytes who moved in his orbit.

"I have a conference next week," Jonathan says. "While I'm gone you can find yourself an apartment and pack your things. If you're worried about money I can leave you a cheque." His voice is still steady, his hand still wrapped calmly around his glass. But Carolyn, listening for it, can sense the change in tone.

"You said you were drinking too much. Maybe you are. Maybe it's time you did something about it. Think about yourself, Jonathan. Think about what you're doing to us." Then she lifts her hand and forces herself to lay her fingers against his chest. Begins stroking him very slowly, very carefully, the way you stroke a puppy or a kitten so that they know you aren't ever going to desert them.

The Romantic

The Romantic

Paolo in his twenties: tall, tweed jacket, grey slacks that hung loosely on his pipe-stem legs, face taut and constantly rippling with surprise, mossy brown hair already receding from a forehead so smooth and round it made everything he said seem droll and ironic, green-blue eyes which would turn muddy with time.

In those days, the prematurely tired and world-weary man you eventually met was barely in embryo. At that time, in fact, Paolo-in-embryo was the opposite of what he would eventually become. Young, Paolo was an energetic cyclone roaming the city in search of a victim. I never made appointments with Paolo; it was easier to find him in the street, suddenly coming up on you just when you didn't expect him, walking too fast, in long jerky strides people lost their breath keeping up with. With this little trick — Paolo's admirers explained to each other — Paolo kept us securely in the role of listeners for his non-stop commentaries on everything from his newest method of deducing the sexual peccadilloes of various professors by reading their body language, to hitherto un-discovered — but absolutely revolutionary in terms of their implications — contradictions in the early works of Marx, Hegel or Bob Dylan. When he was finished Paolo would even give you the book: especially if it was due at the library.

One time, for example — although with Paolo there were never exactly examples but rather a series of one-time-only incidents, little masterpieces of street theatre performed for an audience of one (even if, as it was easy to suspect, Paolo not only prepared these off-the-cuff occasions but counted on them being recounted sufficiently to become part of whatever legend he had in mind: Dant-esque Italian bard transmigrated in space and time, I always thought) — one time I met Paolo as he emerged from the Varsity restaurant on Bloor Street.

Immediately he burst out talking. We were walk-ing west and the afternoon sun was already low enough to be glaring into our eyes. "You won't believe what I've been doing! It's the most fantastic thing. Do you know that I've been writing a novel?"

Even by the time he had finished this introduc-tion Paolo had extracted from his briefcase a thick sheaf of papers from which he began to read. Rake-thin, needing a haircut, declaiming loudly and gesturing for each of the characters, Paolo began putting on such a show that soon there were half a dozen spectators clustered around us. The novel began with the words — "One day the fattest man in the world thought he was hungry . . ."

It's always been my opinion that such a beginning could have led to a masterpiece, had only Paolo continued. In any case the chapters Paolo read to me — to us — that day concerned the adventures of the fattest man in the world as he ambled down the very stretch of Bloor Street we ourselves were travelling. At each restaurant he would stop, attempt to squeeze his tremendous bulk through the door, and if successful proceed to eat vast amounts of ice cream. Each episode Paolo read in front of the restaurant in question. Sometimes this involved standing on the spot for twenty minutes or so while Paolo delineated events I can't now remember. The waitresses in his novel had all been taken from life. At one point a spectator actually went into the chosen palace, a dubious Hispano-Ukrainian joint known as Casa Perogi, and dragged out the waitress so that she could hear herself being described by Paolo as "a greasy-fingered harridan whose lips seemed built for the vacuum extraction of juice from tropical fruit." Don't ask me what happened to his hero in the end. But by the time evening came I was at Paolo's place for dinner. He was living then — as he did for almost twenty years — in one of those apartments above grocery stores where he loved to squat. And to cook. Food on the stove, mistress of the moment perched prettily and listening to his rambling monologues, bottles of cheap Italian wine — *vino rosso*, Paolo would growlingly call it — lined up like so many hours eager to be consumed, Paolo was the centre of the universe.

However, things were never so simple as they seemed. Paolo lied, especially to himself, about himself. He had a case, as a poet from his father's native Trieste once called it, of *bovarysme*. Just as

Madame Bovary mistakenly believed herself a great heroine destined for great love, so Paolo believed himself — but what Paolo believed himself to be was always shifting. Philosopher, novelist, ladies' man, European intellectual manqué, writer of faultless prose, movie critic, leader and pied piper — these were only a few of the incarnations through which Paolo slid.

Dead. How the hand drags writing the word.

I clearly remember Paolo saying to me: "I wouldn't want to suffer for no purpose." He was telling me something, I thought. And as he spoke he looked at me — *significantly*, as they say — his doctor, his friend, his final exit from pain. That was before the disease had fully invaded him, before he had been consigned to his final bed, perhaps even before he realized the implications —

For the final decision I take total responsibility. At the time — doctor, friend — I was doing my duty. Only afterwards arrived the guilt, our own brief frenzies, my gradual collapse into — what? This state of mental decomposition? Or perhaps I am only seized by the need to confess.

"I don't want to die in front of her" were Paolo's last words. You were downstairs in the recently remodelled kitchen, standing beneath the movable track-lights Paolo had himself so carefully installed. There was, you had thought, no particular cause for alarm. "Serene" was the word you later used to describe your mood that evening. You said it hating yourself for not knowing what was to happen — nor do you know yet the actual event which is the excuse for this confession. But we were talking about "serenity." Shall I tell you why you

used that word? Because you were at peace with
yourself, satisfied and victorious. At least Paolo
would have called you victorious, but you claimed
the drugs were pushing him into paranoia. Let's
save the details for later, but the result was that
Paolo instructed, "I don't want to die in front of
her." At the time I was sure those were his words.
Later I wondered. What if he had really mumbled
something else? "I don't want to die before her"; or
even, "I don't want to cry in front of her." For
example, the other day I asked for a ginger ale and
the waiter brought me a Caesar salad. When I
looked puzzled, he said, "Had you wanted the
small?"

The fact is I am a man who has made very few
decisions. This sounds odd but it is not. Even going
to medical school was only a fulfilment of my
parents' wishes. And when I assign a prescription
or a course of treatment, I don't really decide, I only
follow the logic of the symptoms and the tests.

What about my personal life? Those are the
decisions that are supposed to tell. A dutiful Jewish
boy who became a doctor, I also married and, so to
speak, multiplied. Yet now I am divorced. My wife
and child live on the other side of the continent and
my relationship with my daughter is so insubstan-
tial that when my wife offered her to me for a
summer, I was finally afraid to face her. Also there
have been my various adventures with females,
unconsummated and otherwise. But for the latter I
plead action by inaction. Passive, docile, with little
to offer, I have been just a complicit victim slightly
overeager to fall into the arms of the women who
will eventually betray me.

Action by inaction. A great ticket. But it doesn't

apply to Paolo's death; even though in the final medical report — the one I myself wrote with the help of a colleague at the morgue of the Toronto General Hospital — the immediate causes of death were listed as "heart failure complicated by pneumonia and self-administered non-prescribed barbiturates."

Paolo in his thirties: an imposing figure — still tall and erect, pale face growing gaunt and the deep lines that eventually bracketed his mouth already beginning to carve themselves out. But no longer was Paolo a man to be met by chance, nor could he be guaranteed to be found in the spell of a new and unpredictable enthusiasm. In the ten years since the invention of "the fattest man in the world," the irony had turned to sarcasm and cynicism, the racing stride to an efficient lope that sped from office to bar and back again.

But then, just as Paolo threatened to crystallize, he announced that on his thirty-fifth birthday he was getting married. It was strictly romance, total love; Paolo had been struck dumb and dazzled. At the time I couldn't believe you loved him in return. You were a hot-shot philosophy professor who had first made — apparently — an academic reputation in England, then returned to your native wilderness to become a "feminist" television producer shooting through Toronto's tiny media world. Paolo, meanwhile, the prodigal night-prowler, had already started to run out of steam. Shakespeare, Melville, Fellini — who might Paolo not have become? Instead, somehow, when you and he collided, Paolo had started to erode at the centre. Or so I thought, because although we still saw each other frequently I had begun to find — dare I say it? — my admired friend becoming a bore. The girlfriends were changing a little too often, the bottles emptying out of habit rather than good honest greed, and even the monologues were running out of steam. Paolo, inexplicably losing his gifts, had sunk from the clouds and come down to earth as the editor of a city magazine featuring mostly advertisements for waterbeds and such. Poor Paolo, I was beginning to think; at the age when he should have been growing wings, he was growing old, a prematurely tired journalist, a semi-alcoholic who spent his lunches and nights drinking, his weekends screwing the hired help.

But on his wedding day Paolo seemed his old self — idealized version — resurrected. He wore a real tuxedo tailored to show off his tall and surprisingly elegant figure. Even his teeth, freshly cleaned by a dentist and gleaming an uncharacteristic white, seemed to declare that the long detour was over and that Paolo the charming Roman candle was back in town.

To confirm the impression of an over-ripe skin discarded, Paolo announced that he was giving up the last of his grocery-store apartments; the ecstatic new couple would be moving into a to-be-renovated Victorian townhouse. One of those townhouses, it might be said, which forty years ago housed poor immigrants including one from Trieste, Paolo's father, now a wealthy developer living in the suburbs. Much clapping, whistling too. Especially piercing whistles from the wealthy father who himself had married a younger woman following the death of Paolo's mother. As I said in my toast to the groom, "It is a day of endings and of

beginnings — today we wave good-bye to the last of
Toronto's great seedy journalists, but we witness
the birth of a dynamic and forceful couple destined
to rise to the social and financial heights of our
great and beloved world-class metropolis.''

Afterwards there were people, given the courage
of champagne, who said I had been daring, meaning nasty and jealous. But you were sweet. You had
— and still have — that kind of fine-boned delicate
face which, when given to women, seems incapable
of lies, of stupidity, of greed. I thought I knew
better. What future you could see in Paolo escaped
me. I thought you wanted him for a trophy, a safety
net, a way to avoid affairs and liaisons that might
impede your ambition.

All this about Paolo and so little about you? Yes,
I remember you. The strange upside-down U, for
example, made by your arm, your armpit, your
breast (at certain times, in certain positions). The
particular scent of the sweat that always gathered in
the hollows above your narrow hips. The smell of
coffee on your breath. The rough-sweet texture of
your tongue. I could go on with these illegal
memories. I could tell you how years after we
stopped sleeping together I still remember every
touch, every bed, the feel of every sheet that con-
spired with us.

Paolo in his forties: Paolo after a decade of marriage. He was drinking heavily — too heavily — his
face becoming coarse and bloated even while his
thin body grew more skeletal. When he came to
confide his unhappiness to me, his affairs, I was less
than surprised.

You were too rich for him — and I don't mean

wealthy. Too complex, too driven, too protected by
your galaxies of women's emotions, women's ex-
pectations. You won't like my saying this. You'll
protest that I'm underestimating Paolo, that he
could have lived up to you if only he had made the
effort. *It was his decision*, you'll say. *His failure*,
you mean. The truth is that you spotted Paolo's
weakness from the beginning. You thought you
could re-construct him in your image. Perhaps you
didn't want to know that you are the kind of
woman no man can survive.

Have you ever noticed, incidentally, how people's
faces change when they make love? There is a
biological explanation, of course — a redistribu-
tion of blood causing lips to swell, nostrils to flare,
eyes to open wider; but having seen the private face
of love-making, of desire, of total need and total
satisfaction — then the public face is never again
convincing. The face previously so plausible, the
one you saw at the office or at parties is now a stiff
and slightly askew mask ready to yield at a touch to
the real face lurking beneath.

Your face, for example, so composed in public,
so abandoned and needing in bed. How easy it must
have been for men to addict themselves to that need,
to believe the need would continue beyond
nakedness.

You must hate me talking about this. Your own
bovarysme lies in thinking yourself a tight-assed
schoolmarm in a world of lecherous and exploiting
men. And that other side of you, that side of
yourself you have struggled so hard against. Dead
now? After our unexpected tango, did it follow
Paolo to the grave? Or does it still occasionally
explode when you are safely away on holiday?

Paolo confiding his unhappiness to me. He knew about your affairs but didn't blame you. Nor was he as pure and victimized as you thought. He even had a regular, an almost-second wife. She was the actual wife of someone you yourself had a fling with. When she and Paolo deduced the obvious they decided to console each other — and amazingly enough that was what they found. True consolation: a mutual soothing of wounded souls, a mutual refuge from the injuries inflicted by the world and their own weakness. But he never wanted to play house with her. "First of all," Paolo said, "because I love not her but what we have. And secondly, more importantly, because if we had it all the time, we would destroy it. Or I would. And I can't live without it."

Do you know that French wine comes from Dutch pigs? Here is the explanation. The Netherlands is suffering under a tremendous pigshit crisis. This wasn't always so. In fact, no surprise, the pigshit crisis was brought about by politics and success. That is, after the formation of the Common Market Holland suddenly found itself a powerful exporter of pork and pork products. This seemed like a good thing, and all around the countryside pig barns sprouted like giant aluminum tulips. Problem: outside every pig barn, a growing mound of pigshit. And we're talking about a country which is small, a country blessed with marshy land which is fertile, but very unsuited to garbage disposal. Unable to descend, the pigshit began to rise, in the form of ammonia clouds. Soon the infected Dutch sky began to spread pig-acid rain upon its own and neighbouring lands.

Fortunately a solution was found. Since the mountains were not allowed to go to Mohammed, they were turned into small grey pellets and sold to French farmers to fertilize their vineyards.

A Bible full of morals could be drawn from this story, including the reflection that even difficult situations caused by greed don't necessarily have bad endings. But the problem with you and Paolo was that — unlike some happier couples — you never found foreign soil to welcome your little mountains of unhappiness. Create it you did — with your affairs, your continual desire to reform each other. The solution, according to Paolo, was to have children. But you claimed, also according to Paolo, that being a free woman meant ownership of your own body including the right to open or close it at will. I make it sound stupid but in fact — surprise — I agree with you. Freedom unused is freedom lost. If you'd had children right away, you would have ended up the harassed stay-at-home wife of an alcoholic journalist who spent his nights in bars boasting about the wife and family. Perhaps. And, to be fair, when you married Paolo you warned him that you wanted to wait ten years before having children.

Paolo at forty-five: a tall thin man with the spongy skin of a drinker sitting on the examination table wearing baggy jungle-coloured boxer shorts. The night before, he told me, you had announced that the decade had passed and that you wanted to begin bearing his heirs. If he was up to it.

Blood pressure. Pulse. Blood and urine tests. Rectal examination. Cardiogram. X-rays. I also sent him to a urologist who tested his sperm for numbers, swimming skills, longevity.

The results could have been worse. He did not have cancer or any other fatal ailment. His blood sugar, it was true, was undesirably volatile. Possible disorder of the pancreas, even future diabetes if he didn't drink less. Prostate slightly but not yet dangerously enlarged. Heart very strong. Amazingly. He told me proudly that he had started playing squash twice a week. He was surprised when I replied that his heart was supporting the exercise and not vice versa.

"If I have a child?" he asked me. "Will I leave him an orphan before he's ten?"

"Probably not," I could honestly say. And then added, always conscientious, that what he had to watch was the drinking.

"I drink because I'm unhappy," Paolo pouted. His legs were absolute bones, but he had a small pot-belly. Easy for me to imagine the organs swollen and distended inside.

"You drink because you drink. Don't lie to yourself."

When the results came back from the urologist we had a happier conversation. "Don't tell me over the phone," Paolo insisted, "come round to my office after work."

By the time Paolo started coming to me for his medical problems we were no longer friends in the way we had been. Close? Yes. Every few months I would come to your place — with one or another of my showcase companions — for an awkward little evening during which Paolo behaved impeccably and you pretended to enjoy yourself. More often, when you went away on business for example, Paolo would call on me to join him for a long alcoholic dinner. Enjoyable to reminisce. But the webs were spun around the past not the future and if — when the restaurant had emptied and the bottle of cognac had been brought to stay at our table — Paolo ventured to talk about himself, then suddenly we were floating softly around fresh wounds. Paolo the magnificent inventor of the fattest man in the world was in danger of becoming one of his own grotesque creations. "If I hated myself," he said once, "it would be because I might not have the courage to walk away."

But that evening in his office Paolo was flying again. Or at least floating with his long legs up on the desk, his chair swivelled to share with me his skyscraper view of the city skyline as I happily reported that he was an absolute sultan of swat, a menace to any fertile female within shooting distance: "All you have to do is get it up and get it in."

"No problem, doc," Paolo beamed, and then out of the cupboard came a bottle of Jamieson's to toast the little ones to come.

But we were talking about pigshit and wine. Self-inflicted acid rain. Environmental damage. Things gone too far. All the years of birth control had proved self-fulfilling — now your doctor discovered scarred tubes and a semi-functional womb.

"Tough luck," Paolo grunted, when I relayed the news from the specialists. This time we were at your house and, for the bad news as for the good, a bottle was produced.

"There's always the outside chance," I told you. You were crying. Because, I thought at the moment, you had misjudged yourself and now realized you had wanted children all along. But I was wrong, again. You were crying because you loved Paolo and couldn't bear to disappoint him.

Scenes I can't bear to describe in detail:

One: At the funeral, where I am in the row behind you, the sun is coldly bright and the swirling wind makes the sound of traffic rise and fall like a moaning animal. I move closer to you. The sun has turned your untanned skin into pale transparent porcelain. I think of Paolo in his coffin. Not the ideal Paolo but the actual Paolo. Gutted and embalmed. Skin beginning to collapse and rot. Cornea-less eyes staring into their lids. Brain intact. With death comes desire.

Two: On Richard's fourth birthday, just a couple of months before the funeral, I drop by the house with a present for the miracle baby. A pirate suit. It is eleven in the morning. Richard answers the door naked. "I'm four," he screams. And then: "I'm going on a trip." "Where?" "Penis-and-bum country," he shrieks, turns, gives me the moon, then runs upstairs laughing wildly.

Three: Me leaning over you, working late into the night, my arms aching. And I am thinking this is exactly the way it was, leaning over Paolo, my arms aching, pushing the pillow into his face while with what life remained those long legs kicked and flailed.

Four: Me alone in my house. Me filling the syringe for the first time. Me putting the needle to my own vein, wanting to close my eyes.

Five: Me coming to consciousness after the first blackout. I am lying on my office floor. The telephone is ringing and I hear the answering service: "Doctor Weinstein is presently in conference. Please leave your name and telephone number so he can get back to you as soon as he is able."

Paolo's father came to see me one afternoon. This was when you were already pregnant with Richard. He is over eighty now, so he must have been in his late seventies then. Still a handsome, well set-up man. Shorter than Paolo, wider and bigger boned. A big man in an expensive striped blue suit. Tinted sunglasses, a cane mostly for effect, hands swollen and spotted. He was happy for Paolo, he said. He knew I was his close friend, his doctor, almost his guardian angel, and now that Paolo was starting a family, he wanted, he said, to give him some of the money he would eventually inherit. He was afraid that Paolo would refuse unless another party, someone like myself for example, he said, somehow made things easier.

Paolo's father was — like his son — a handsome man. The blue-eyed fair northern Italian look; but in the father it seemed to have flowered before fading whereas with Paolo it corroded from the inside.

Paolo has lots of money, I told him. He and his wife have very successful careers; you wouldn't believe how much money people make these days, despite what you read in the papers.

"You can't make him take it?" his father asked.

"You could start a trust for the child."

This made the old man feel better, though it wasn't what he wanted. That evening I had dinner at your place. You were already showing. You wore a blue linen dress with white piping that made you look like a little girl in a sailor suit. Pregnancy had made you vulnerable, soft, eager for Paolo's love.

The way Paolo had always wanted you to be. And he had somehow lost his bitter, complaining edge. In the kitchen, juice glass in one hand and wooden stirring spoon in the other, he was an aging but happy version of his younger self. Pots bubbled over like enthusiastic cartoons; immaculately-presented dishes appeared. Everything was ship-shape, cosy, the triumph of a marriage that had endured.

When you were pregnant you ate so much of Paolo's food that your throat grew thicker, your chin threatened to double, your smile was framed by an extra set of dimples. Even your arms gained weight; watching you hold your tea that night — we were eating in our favourite place, the kitchen, candle-lit — I saw the flesh on your forearm had a new and voluptuous curve. The sweet hormones of pregnancy are showing, I dared to say to Paolo. He kissed the soft skin inside your elbow, ran his tongue along to your wrist. Before you were preg-nant you had hated that sort of public thing: now you held out your other arm for the same treatment — a few minutes later I left so that you and he could go to bed. Do you remember? And do you remem-ber the first place that I kissed you? The cradle of desire, I called that soft and foldy skin. You didn't know why and I was ashamed to explain the birth of my own feelings for you. So I told you another truth, which is that your skin there is supremely sweet and silky. Compared to what? you asked, and so I kissed not only the insides of your elbows but the backs of your knees, the webbed skin between your fingers and toes, the lobes of your ears, the sharp corners of your eyes; and so on.

I kiss. I am kissed. Therefore I exist.

But the night that I glimpsed the cradle of desire I was thinking not of my need for you but of Paolo's. In your kitchen, multi-paned glass doors turning the half-dozen candles into a host of burning spears, you in your vulnerable dress. Paolo melting with love — you two were my burning oases in the darkness. Darkness, yes. Death, fear of death, desire for death, obsession with death, were and are the ruling stars of both my personal and professional lives. Or did you take me as I seemed? A dry, self-possessed, self-contained man leading a dry, sensible life lubricated by a few well-chosen but undemanding female accomplices to share my opera tickets, my trips to the art gallery, my seasonal weekends in New York. Stiff reliable Marcus.

But that night with you and Paolo, I understood again, again, that for Paolo death was not a factor. Unhappiness, yes. Oblivion — if self-administered and poured from a bottle. But for Paolo there would always be a next morning, a chance to wake up to a better world. Paolo knew how to hope! For years he went to the track on Friday afternoons, this was before he met you, because merely betting on a horse — having the chance to believe that the unfortunate nag he'd wagered on was about to accelerate out of its lethargy and zoom to the front of the pack — was in itself enough to make him happy. With you, too, his loveliest and most beloved, he placed his bets. It took him almost ten years to realize that he was going to keep losing — every day, every way. And then, just as faith was destroyed, it was restored. No happier man than Paolo.

For the record: a few lines ago it was afternoon. I
was sitting in my office, the sun on my back, the
outer door locked, the phone routed to the answering service. In my womb — warm, glassy, soporific.
And with the sun to give me courage I could write
about magic evenings, golden oases in the
blackness.

Now the sun has hidden behind an office building and I am writing by the white glare of my table
lamp. You'll be glad to know that as always I'm
wearing a suit — the black wool one, in fact, that
you helped me choose during our brief interlude,
but I'm afraid I've had to unbutton my shirt and
take off my tie. Kick off my shoes? That would be
going too far. In any case my shoes are handmade,
shaped by expert fingers to soothe my feet. We
doctors have to find ways to enjoy our money. To
tell the truth, what I really wish is that you would
walk through the door. What would I prefer, I often
ask myself: to be with you in our first bed, starting
off again on our first voyage of discovery; or to live
in an alternate universe, the penis-and-bum country where you and Richard and Paolo still live in
love's hotel?

We were talking about Paolo in his coffin. I was the
one, you will remember, who had to make the
choice because you said you couldn't bear to. "Get
the most expensive one," you instructed me. A
young undertaker — sympathetic, good-looking,
not unctuous — led me to the display room. Piped-
in music softly played, breaking a silence that
would otherwise have been absolute. Like one of
the high-rise waiting-rooms to which the soul of
the departed had doubtless already ascended. The

displayed coffins were all open, ready to receive.

You had wanted me to choose the most expensive, but that multi-coloured number was less a coffin than an ark. And so I decided Paolo would be satisfied with a cherry-wood treasure box whose surface had been worked and polished to a fine shining velvet. Along the sides ran sturdy rails, a useful concession to mortal pallbearers. Stainless steel reinforcements guaranteed that even organized armies of worms would not be able to pry open the lid. Inside was a contoured "resting place." Upholstered in shining scarlet satin, it was the kind of coffin into which you should wear a white leather suit and cowboy boots. I said this to the young undertaker. "Leather lasts," he said. "I could show you something in leather if you like."

We buried Paolo in his wedding suit. And the inside of his coffin was re-done in white. The sensitive undertaker deserves credit for that, also for lengthening the inside to fit Paolo by removing some of the padding at his feet. "You know, doctor, a man's at his longest lying down," he reminded me. "Might as well get comfortable in the driver's seat."

So there's Paolo, riding on white satin, but he's going nowhere. He was in bad shape when we buried him but his state must be more than serious by now. You would think that some time in my life as a medical student or doctor I would have had occasion to see such people. It's even true that for a few months I played with the idea of being a medical detective. But in the end I was too squeamish. So Paolo's gradual melt-down is as indistinct a nightmare to me as it is to you. One difference: in the past few months you have suddenly become a

believer, trotting off to church for absolution at
every opportunity. Whereas I, alas, am even less
inspired than ever. On the day of Paolo's funeral I
imagined his intact brain still functioning away
and reporting to itself the gruesome state of affairs.
Now, even though the individual cells must have
long ago begun to merge, and though the electrical
connections must be growing worse than rusty, I
can't help but think that Paolo's brain — in some
drunken nightmarish way — must be recording its
own gradual dissolution into nothingness.

Paolo dead. But the undertaker was right: he *is* in
the driver's seat, driving us. Of course, even though
our relationship has returned to its old frozen
footing, we still see each other. You try to seem
friendly when I come to pick up Richard for a
baseball or a hockey game. Last Saturday — did he
tell you? — I took him for a drive in the country
and showed him the small town where your parents
used to live before they moved to Florida. He
wanted to see your old school, so we searched
around, finding only a very modern-looking insti-
tute complete with Olympic-size community pool.

I also drove him, not so far away from the town,
to a road near Lake Simcoe where you can walk
along the water for a few hundred yards until the
beach ends at a series of private cottages. He seemed
to like that — being out of the city, the fresh air, the
sight of the lake. I didn't tell him that I've bought
one of the cottages, a place with a nice shallow
beach overhung by trees so he can learn to swim
without getting skin cancer.

Of course you'll have to come with us but I'm not
expecting anything from you. In fact, what I imagine is mild torture: while Richard happily splashes

in the water, me watching over him, you'll be
stretched out on a lawnchair, more oblivious than
ever, your eyes hidden behind your oversized sunglasses and your mind happily imprisoned in the
bubble of those paperback novels you can never get
enough of. Black one-piece bathing suit. Tanned
legs. A few stray hairs peeking out at the seam
where suit and skin join at inner thigh. Will
reading these descriptions of yourself make you
uncomfortable? I don't want you to think I am
fascinated only by your private parts. In the line of
hair, for example, I like equally the hair on your
arms, the neat and orderly way it lies in parallel
rows. Also the transparent down that follows the
curve of your jawbone. Even the single black strand
that grows from the mole behind your left shoulder.

Your voice. "She has the sexiest voice," Paolo told
me. Do I think so? Of course, fifteen years have
passed since Paolo made his observation. And
barely a minute since I have actually heard your
voice. In fact, if you'll pardon the slightly obscene
image, I was still holding the pen as we talked. At
various times during our conversation your voice
sounded to me — I merely transcribe here what I
jotted down at the moment — inviting, cold,
hostile, vulnerable, desperate, business-like, bitter,
matter-of-fact, holey. "Holey" is the key one. I
mean that your voice is riddled with little holes, an
ambivalent veil wanting at the same time to hide
and to be seen through. But what is it you want me
to see? Not, I hardly think, the flesh-and-blood
creature who is constantly peeking out from behind
the protective devices. Despite your worst thoughts
about me, you would be horrified to read these

pages, to know that while you have been presenting me with your impermeable lacquered self, I have been searching for stray hairs and glimpses of desire. Pervert! Lecher! Enemy of civilization! Infantilism at its worst. The kind of man who fastens his eyes on your breasts as you walk down the street. (Here I exaggerate, I admit — now that I think of it — I wonder which would annoy you more: the idea that I am always trying to see your breasts or the prospect of my complete disinterest? How can I be writing this down? I ask myself.)

"Are you busy this evening?" Your voice: inviting, cool, hostile, etc.

"No," I say. Though it seems to me that I've been sitting here forever, writing forever, and that the task of writing stretches forward into infinity.

"Would you like to come to dinner?" A slight pause and then, to explain it: "Richard says there's a game on television."

"That would be very nice," I say. The morning our — affair? interlude? carnal holiday? — ended was the morning I slept over unintentionally and Richard came in the door, stopped when he saw me in your and Paolo's bed, turned and left. We were only dozing. A few naked parts but nothing serious sticking out from under the sheets. What Richard saw or didn't see we never discussed. The curtain, as they say, fell.

"Around seven-thirty or are you working late?"

"Seven-thirty would be perfect. Can I bring anything?"

"Just yourself."

Another pause. "Always the perfect hostess," I think. Or perhaps I say it. The problem is that as the seconds pile up, I can remember less and less whether I actually heard the sound of my own voice, slightly sarcastic as always with you, or if I only imagined uttering the words and am now imagining that you are refusing to rise to the bait.

The silence continues. If I actually did say "always the perfect hostess," it was a terrible gaffe: in any case it is now your turn to talk. If I didn't say it then, the gaffe I imagined but didn't utter is now being replaced by a new embarrassment — the fact that I'm saying nothing when it is *my* turn to talk.

"Just yourself." Those were your exact words. I wrote them down. What do you say to someone after they say "just yourself"? Aside from "always the perfect" etc. "I'm never alone when I'm with you," I consider trying. Even after I imagine it, I can't hear the sound of my own voice. So I'm absolutely certain *those* words weren't spoken. Just as well. But I can hear you breathing. Time is passing. The pressure is building. You, of course, know what agony I am in. Playing it straight is your method of revenge. You're sure that sooner or later I'm going to crack.

"It's not so easy," I say. Meaning it's not so easy to break me down. But you take it the wrong way — first another eternal pause and then, as if you too are writing down the words and examining them in order to misconstrue them, you reply as if I've asked for sympathy.

"It's not easy for me either," you say. Tones of forgiveness. Accusation. Most of all your special kind of holey-ness through which I am supposed to glimpse — But what are you trying to tell me?

"I know," I say. Reverting to my bedside manner. "See you later." It sounds like this case requires a housecall, I add in my mind, then realize as my voice dies away that this time I definitely did say the wrong thing.

You laugh.

Midnight or later. Richard in bed. You too are probably asleep. And I am thinking of you, or at least thinking that sooner or later these pages will fall into your hands. You'll bend over them, slightly hunched, the way you always position yourself to read. This last year, it is almost the exact anniversary of Paolo's death, you've been letting your hair grow, letting the grey show. So you'll be veiled as you absorb this blasphemy. Obscenity. Defacement of the grave. By now you know I killed Paolo. Held the pillow over his face — not as easy as you would think, incidentally, or maybe you didn't think it would be easy — fought back my tears as he kicked and struggled — I was terrified that with the thumping of his feet I wouldn't hear you come into the room and catch us at it.

But we were talking about you. About how you'll feel when you read this. Exhilarated? Shattered? Bored? The better we get to know each other, the more I see of you, the less I feel I understand you. Crazy thought. Crazy where I am writing it, here at Paolo's desk, in Paolo's study in the made-over attic of your stylish little townhouse. In this attic Paolo and I used to sometimes listen to music and drink after you had gone to bed. In the summer we would sit on the deck outside. Do you remember, three years ago, when after his bout with chemotherapy Paolo made his brave excursion into theatre and wrote that play? It got panned by the only newspaper that reviewed it. And do you remember the night the three of us sat drinking mournfully on

this deck until you had to go to sleep? After that
Paolo took out his telescope and, instead of pointing it at the stars, showed me that he had a direct
line of sight to the house where the theatre critic
lived. We aimed at his windows. Surprise! The
Paolo-basher and his wife were stripping for bed.
Raddled fallen flesh, pot bellies, curved spines; they
looked like senile hairless apes. Worse — it was
hard to tell who was who — one of them lay on top
of the other and they started to have some kind of
intercourse. Paolo hooked up the special camera he
had bought for taking bird pictures and recorded
the entire event. The instant that the last gasp had
been gasped and the last shutter clicked, we went to
the hospital and got one of the technicians to
develop the photographs. Nice and large. Full
contrast. We picked the most disgusting dozen, put
them into a classic "plain brown envelope" and
drove to the house where Paolo slid it through the
mail slot. What he did with the negatives I don't
know — I always expected them to turn up when
you went through his papers after the funeral.

Eighteen minutes past one. Why am I writing
this down? I ask myself. Which reminds me of a
joke I heard in the operating-room the other day.
Why do some men pee in the corner? Answer:
because that way they can splash two walls at once.
Not that this confession is the equivalent, exactly,
but perhaps I'm writing it so that you'll have to
share the burden I've been carrying alone.

After I killed Paolo I closed his eyes, then I
rushed to the head of the stairs and called out to
you. By the time you arrived, hurrying, panicked,
by the time we had reached the door of the bedroom, it was of course too late. While you watched I

took his pulse. You were sobbing; grief and relief mixed, I imagine. I too was crying. You kept looking at me as though I was supposed to do something else, so finally I took his arms out from under the covers and crossed them neatly on top.

Then I telephoned the hospital. With one exception things took their official and inevitable course. The exception: I had assumed you would want the body immediately removed from the house to the undertaker's. But you insisted that Richard have a last look. You woke him up, you told him the sad news, in his state of sleepy shock you carried him to the darkened room and gave him his last sight of his father at home. I was left to deal with the others. When they had gone, and the body had been removed, I came upstairs to tell you that I, too, would be leaving now. You were sitting on your bed, Richard cradled in your arms.

"I'm afraid to be alone tonight," you said. "Would you mind staying?" And so I did. First waiting until you had returned Richard to his bed. Then sitting with you in the living-room, playing Paolo's favourite records. Next morning the light had a pale fleshy colour. You had fallen asleep in Paolo's armchair. I took away your undrunk whisky, covered you with a blanket. When Richard woke up crying I was the one who heard him, the one who had to go upstairs to tell him the nightmare was true.

I carried him down to you. I made breakfast. I helped you explain to Richard that his father's illness had slowly changed him, emptied him, that death was a blessing.

I've opened the window. The wood squeaks with disuse as a cool wind smelling sweetly of spring sweeps into the attic, carrying the sound of rain falling on the new leaves of the oak tree outside the window.

I brought wine for supper tonight. All through the meal you kept mentioning Paolo's name. At first naturally: "Paolo liked baseball" or "Paolo was the one who made me try these dishes." Then you couldn't stop. You were looking at me distressed, afraid of upsetting Richard. Afterwards we watched the baseball game, passing the bottle back and forth to refill our empty glasses while Richard and I talked about batting averages and you worked away blue-pencilling your week's accumulation of scripts.

Amazing how well you have succeeded, given the past years spent as either Paolo's nurse or Paolo's widow. By the time the game was over and Richard in bed, we had not, despite the bottle passing, finished the wine.

"Paolo would have been ashamed of us," you say. And then: "Would you like something different? A liqueur? Tea? Coffee?"

"Tea," I say. I'm thirsty tonight, but not for alcohol. Have you ever noticed that we both always refer fondly to Paolo's drinking? Even though he died of liver cancer. But we never blame Paolo for his own death, although if anyone ever drank himself into the grave — even if he did stop for a couple of years — it was surely he. We don't blame him for his death and we don't blame ourselves for having been his accomplices. If we blame Paolo for anything, it is for leaving us shipwrecked on this strange planet where we have only each other to grasp for survival.

It was in the kitchen that you made your move.

Or we fell together. We ended up doing it in the living-room, like teenagers on the couch. As always you were voluptuous, needy, irresistible. I kept having the feeling that from out in the nothing-ness one of Paolo's cornea-less eyes was trained on us through the telescope that joins life and death, that every frenzied second of our congress was being imprinted into his dissolving brain.

Afterwards we found ourselves in a tangle of half-divested clothes, embarrassments — and yet, and yet: even now my belly is still sticky with you, my hands still smell of you, a sweet dragging tiredness pulls at me inside.

You took off the rest of your clothes, wrapped yourself in a blanket. I pulled up my pants, tucked in my shirt.

"I've never seen you naked," you say. "Not really."

From the kitchen we can hear the electric kettle turning itself on and off. We follow the sound, but my hand reaches instead for the bottle of scotch. Part way through our first drink we are at each other again. This time we go upstairs. Everything happens in slow motion — like the last dance at a masquerade. When it's over we'll discover that we were making love in a ballroom full of ghosts.

"Do you want to stay?" you ask me afterwards. "You can stay here. I'm sure Richard has guessed by now."

But no, I can't. I say that we must tell him first, soon. Declaring this I try to imagine various con-versations — they all seem ludicrous. Then, finally, standing at your door, a long calm embrace that means as much to me as everything that has preceded it. I go downstairs, gather up my suit-jacket and my indispensable doctor's bag, climb the stairs again, wave to you now sitting up in bed wearing some frilly little number Paolo must have bought you for late-night reading — then continue on my way upstairs until I am here, in the attic, sitting at Paolo's desk writing ever more slowly as my thoughts wash along in the rain, falling now hard and heavy.

Extract from a confidential report submitted to the Office of the Attorney General of the Province of Ontario:

> *The enclosed document was found in the inside suit-jacket pocket of Dr Marcus Weinstein. According to the Office of the Coroner, City of Toronto, Dr Weinstein died as the result of a fatal dose of heroin at approximately 3:40 A.M., April 18, 1987. The autopsy further revealed that the victim was a frequent user, possibly an addict. The coroner noted that the injection was probably self-administered, but that whether or not Dr Weinstein was aware of its consequences could not be established. The body of Dr Weinstein was found in the attic bedroom of his late friend, Paolo Antonioni. No charges are contemplated with respect to either the death of Dr Marcus Weinstein or that of Mr Antonioni.*

Living on Water

Living on Water

They are in a restaurant, Maurice and Judith. The restaurant is called "Luciano" and is good enough to have been mentioned, with a knife and a fork, in the red Michelin guide to Italy.

"Would you like a local wine?" the waiter enquires.

"Please," Judith says, as though only an idiot would order anything else. Judith is a poet who has published books and given readings to university students. Her specialty is love poems, sharp jabbing unrhymed sequences about men who do nasty things to women. Over the two years of their relationship Maurice has learned to know her poetry the way one learns the street names of a new city. For a while she even wrote poems about him and the sharp jabbing things he did to her. Maurice was embarrassed, then he learned to like the idea of himself as a dangerous sex criminal on the loose. After her book of poems about Maurice, Judith wrote another book, still love poems, but this time the men were more diffuse. At first Maurice thought he must have grown, in her imagination, to the universal man; next he thought she was using this vagueness as a screen to write about her previous lovers; finally he realized she was starting to write about the lovers she would have after he was gone. Judith denied this. She was also a photographer and one of their most violent fights occurred when Maurice found a sequence of photographs showing him naked and asleep. In these photographs he did not look like a Chairman of the History Department at an important Toronto Secondary School. He looked like an old wino. He was unshaven, his mouth was slack and almost drooling, his modest pot belly sagged to one side and lay beneath his ribs like an unnecessary pillow. There was an exhibition of these photographs and Maurice was glad his parents were not alive to hear about it. One of the pictures was even published in the paper; it was cropped so that his genitals were hidden, but his thin white-fringed face lolled at a strange angle as though he had been decapitated by old age and senility.

The bottle arrives. The waiter sniffs the cork and pours himself a glass which he tests. Maurice remembers an article saying wine from this particular region of Italy has its colour reinforced by dried bull's blood and skim milk powder. During the first course he notices that at every one of the surrounding tables is a couple composed of an elderly man and a young woman. All of the elderly men speak Italian very well, like himself, but their accents betray them as foreigners. All the younger women have the air of being faithful and adoring.

During their main course a man comes in, alone, and sits at the only empty table in the restaurant. Aggressively he places his own red Michelin on the linen cloth. And despite the fact that he immediately orders two pasta dishes, both specialties of the region, he takes only mineral water, without bubbles.

Following the wine Maurice and Judith drink two glasses of Nocino, a heavy black liqueur made by placing green walnuts into containers of alcohol which are left to ferment in the sun for forty days. Coming out of the restaurant, not exactly drunk, but veiled, he stumbles through the narrow streets with Judith on his arm, almost forgotten. Twice they stop to admire churches already inspected by day, and both times Maurice is aware of his Nocino-thickened blood labouring through his veins. Instead of looking at the churches Maurice listens to his lungs wheezing like a waterlogged accordion, and imagines the stately procession of other elderly gentlemen, each with their canes in one hand, their temporary wives in the other, slowly marching back to their respective hotel rooms, where like beautifully embalmed corpses they are laid out on their respective beds, their respective cheeks powdered, their respective lips kissed, their respective eyes closed.

The sound of a fighter plane, a hard tearing noise that ripped apart the sky, woke him up. He had been dreaming of a small spring-fed lake where he had once owned a cottage. In the dream he had driven to the cottage in an unfamiliar car, then stepped down from the car and walked to the beach. The beach was white sand and rock: clearly marked on the rock was the line where the water used to be. Now it had receded several feet, turning the lake into a pond.

"It's still good for swimming," a familiar voice said. Maurice turned to see an old friend from his cottaging years. Then the new owner, the man who had bought the cottage from Maurice, appeared. He had grey hair, a pocked weather-beaten face that had been friendly, almost unctuous when the sale was being arranged but now was bitter and sour, clearly displeased that Maurice had reappeared. But he nodded to Maurice and then, finally, extended his hand. He was wearing a checked shirt and the kind of gabardine pants favoured by the nearby general store that also sold frozen vegetables and live bait.

"You're back," he said.

Maurice couldn't remember his name. "Just visiting."

"The lake went down."

"Swimming is still good."

Other neighbours drifted up to join them. Gradually Maurice felt himself loosening up, the old ties of friendship and love forming again as though he were a stray sheep being re-absorbed into the flock.

It was a bright afternoon, the sun so strong in the blue sky that it shone right through the shallow water to illuminate the entire bottom of the lake. This was white and sandy, as perfectly clean as the most sanitary aquarium, absolutely devoid of plants and fish.

"Beautiful day," one of the neighbours said. He offered Maurice a cigarette and Maurice accepted, thinking that thus was rural life, smoking the product of the land instead of inhaling the soot of cities and the exhausts of a hundred thousand cars. They were all standing together, their arms around one another's shoulders, and Maurice was even thinking of explaining to them that such a brilliant day would be excellent for the fermenting of Nocino — if only they lived in Italy — when the fighter planes began streaking overhead, barely visible black insects exploding across the sky.

He lay in the perfect darkness of the hotel room, fragments of the dream slowly floating to the surface. He was absolutely sober. Beside him Judith was sleeping. Maurice climbed carefully out of bed and walked to the bathroom for a drink. He felt elated. Then he lay down again and stared contentedly up into the blackness. The dream had brought a thin layer of sweat to his skin. As it dried he felt agreeably cool, the kind of coolness that follows a summer swim, the temperature of sanity and clearmindedness. That such a strong reaction could follow a dream was no surprise to Maurice. Two or three times in his life he had experienced dreams equally vivid, equally forceful. Those dreams he had always remembered in great detail, the way some of his friends used to talk about their experiences with drugs or psychiatrists or, in one case, but this was an exception, a friend claimed his own life had reached its watershed the night he spent with a prostitute in Buffalo — "she really knew what to do," the friend had said.

As he settled into this mood of total serenity, Maurice let his mind centre on the dream again, the cottage and the friends. It was coming to him, very slowly, that the cottage he had dreamed was not the one he'd owned with Eleanor but an entirely separate one — one unknown to him in his ordinary life, and that even the friends to whose touch he'd so gladly warmed were complete strangers to his waking hours.

At fifty-three Maurice Rossiter was a thin-faced man with full lips, too-sharp blue eyes, square even teeth, a fringe of white beard. His moustache, also white, curved around his upper lip in an abbreviated handlebar. When he smiled the combined effect was that of one of those wiry white-blue monkeys whose faces are always telling us something we can't understand.

His parents came from a village south of London, and preceding his parents had been, of course, grandparents, and before them, an ever-widening stream of forebears going back, on his father's side, to certain green and misty marshes in Wales. During his moments of ancestor worship Maurice Rossiter pictured them painted blue and dancing out their rituals in front of a roaring fire. At various critical moments in his life Maurice had wished he too could have a bellyful of fermented honey, skin crackling with dye, genitals hanging free, and be lost in the thunder of feet stamping on soft trampled grass.

His mother, Lillian Rossiter, had been born Lillian Silver — an English Catholic by upbringing, but according to family legend the Silvers had been Jewish artisans on the north coast of Spain before fleeing the Inquisition. So while his Welsh ancestors did their merry dance, Maurice supposed, his Hebrew genes were being carried by his other ancestors in the desert, sadly wandering about and awaiting instructions from their God. Such seasons, too, Maurice had known. And sometimes it seemed to him that his life was little more than a pendulum doomed to swing forever between these two extremes.

His parents' view of themselves was less exciting. Lillian, for example, considered herself a woman of culture. In England she had read socialists' novels and the works of George Bernard Shaw. Then she and George — Rossiter, not Shaw — emigrated to Canada. It was the year of the Great Crash and, as George liked to remind his son after a few drinks, Maurice was conceived during the steerage-class journey to Montreal.

"Oh, George," Lillian would cough out, "What are you telling the poor child." She was a director of amateur theatricals and Maurice interpreted her protest as an aesthetic one: she didn't want the children imagining their parents committing "the sacred act" in a cabin crowded with other passengers.

"Those were the days" was always George's reply. "*Tempus fugit.*" The thought of the parents huffing and puffing in the dark, even a populated dark, always raised a laugh from the children, but Maurice had his eye on a different part of the picture. He was watching the steady rivers of sperm struggling to find an egg to mate with. He would imagine the sperm, cute and tiny little tadpoles, racing to accomplish the embryonic embrace. Some might be cheaters, trying to succeed by blocking the others; some would rely on sprinting to victory, thrashing away at the head of the pack; finally there would be the marathon sperms, the wise distance-runners pacing themselves for the long haul. Meanwhile, serenely watching the Celtic dance of the sperm, the egg — a Hebrew Cleopatra barge of life — would be floating down the fallopian Nile.

During the depression the Rossiters lived in Edmonton, which had more sun than money. When Maurice finally went to university, a scholarship boy, he reversed his parents' direction and went East: first to the University of Toronto where he studied history, and then all the way back to England where he did his graduate work and revisited the places his parents had talked about.

On his return to Canada he began teaching high school, a serious young man with a slightly Bohemian beard and an acquired English accent to match. He might have been one of those high school bachelors who grow successively thicker crops of dandruff each year, but he was rescued from this fate by Eleanor Hanson, a striking young woman who conceived an inconceivable passion for the bearded young man with a library full of first editions of the British poets.

At this time in his life, his late twenties and early thirties, Maurice supposed himself to be happy. His parents were still alive — there was a brief but obligatory migration west each summer — and his wife showered him with the kinds of attentions he had never expected.

A decade passed in this fashion. There were no children. And then Eleanor Hanson Rossiter turned to someone else, someone close, a computer engineer who was their neighbour at the cottage they rented every August during the ten years of their marriage.

In a certain indirect way, Maurice had seen it coming. That is, while the exquisite August evenings whittled down towards September, Maurice had noticed Eleanor growing ever more friendly with the computer engineer while the engineer's wife grew ever more sullen.

Over the next few months Maurice's hair turned from black to white. His parents said it looked distinguished but Maurice felt that fate was sending him a message, a message he didn't want to hear, not yet. Instead he concentrated on his hatred of Eleanor. Eleanor's large rubbery breasts squeezed flat by her bathing suit. Those and others of her parts in the hands of her engineer. Eleanor mocking him, using him, discarding him. So he consoled or perhaps revenged himself with what seemed to be an amazing supply of young and willing women. Amazing considering that he had nothing to offer — or at least nothing that he wanted to offer. Then the year Maurice turned forty-five, his parents were killed in an automobile accident.

The news came by telephone, from his sister. When he hung up he found he was crying uncontrollably, and the woman he was with — a colleague from the guidance department who was not even a "girlfriend" but just a fellow member of the Teachers' Union over at his place to help with a report — began crying with him. It was a total collapse, an instant unstoppable nervous breakdown, and for the next few weeks the only adult he could bear to speak to was this spinsterish colleague he had not even slept with. Finally he realized he had become completely dependent on her. And so he said to this woman — to himself he was already calling her "the innocent victim" — that he would like to go a month without seeing her, in order to think about their future.

After a couple of weeks Maurice found himself missing her desperately. Sometimes she would telephone him, and though he never telephoned her, he always welcomed her calls and spent long hours exchanging gossip and personal news, all the while tempted to cancel the whole absurd experiment. Until the telephones were once more on their cradles and he was alone in his apartment, the same one he had shared with Eleanor, though missing most of the furniture and the art, looking out on the lights of the city and trying to measure the exact extent of his loneliness and pain.

On one of those nights the telephone rang, but it was Eleanor. After a few introductory remarks about the divorce Eleanor invited him to come to her apartment for a drink. Unthinking, Maurice accepted.

When he pressed the buzzer and identified himself into the intercom he was so nervous he was barely able to squeeze his name out of his constricted throat. And when Eleanor opened the door — more lipstick than he remembered, larger nose, too, but also smaller breasts, he felt so dizzy with sexual excitement that he found himself hanging onto the door-frame to steady himself while she gave him that wise insincere Chiclet smile she had used so frequently during the last years of their marriage.

"You're looking great," she said, "but I was expecting you to be more tanned."

This was a reference to the trip Maurice had made to the Bahamas during Christmas break with a girlfriend.

"It rained," Maurice said. "We had to stay inside."

Eleanor blinked, like a boxer who has been unexpectedly nailed with a sharp jab. Then the smile came back.

"Too bad you never liked to screw," she said.

Then she laughed, a real laugh, and Maurice laughed with her: this was another of Eleanor's tricks, one she had perfected since the night she had confessed about the engineer. The idea was that they were two old pros, worldly, their bodies and minds had been through the mill, but all in all they were still friends, because when you've seen someone over toast and coffee for ten years . . .

"You want a drink? Or are you still living on water?"

"Coffee," Maurice said. "If it isn't too late."

Soon he was sitting in his old armchair, feet up on the hassock where he had rested them a decade ago — when marriage was still new, when the computer engineer was a shadow in the future instead of the past, when he was too innocent to know that a few drinks and a few loose screws could separate his feet from his furniture for years at a time.

"Your health," Eleanor said. As he turned his eyes up to her face he noticed that he had been sitting with his shoulders hunched forward, his chin down, and that at the same moment he had been lifting up his cup he had been lowering his head, so that he was drinking his coffee the way that his father used to eat his soup — lowering his head towards spoon and bowl with his neck curved like a dog too often beaten.

"How's the new girlfriend? Or do you have a girlfriend these days?"

"Nothing serious," Maurice said.

"You were always the bachelor type. I don't know what attracts me to you guys. There must be something wrong with me."

Then she had lit a cigarette, offering one to Maurice.

"I guess you're wondering why I telephoned you."

"I was wondering," Maurice said, though he hadn't been. Instead he'd been noticing that the sexual excitement he had felt entering the apartment had by now almost completely translated itself into an unwelcome buzzing through the marrow of his bones, a slightly nauseating sensation that made him want to leave. "I thought you must want to talk about the divorce."

"That's it," Eleanor said. Then she stood up and crossed the room until she was in front of Maurice. For a moment she hesitated, as if unsure what to do. Then she knelt in front of him, the way she used to years ago, before they were married and she used to joke that the chairs weren't close enough. She put her hands on his knees and then, her face contorting, she leaned forward so that her face was between his thighs. Maurice watched his hand as, unable to stop itself, it tentatively reached out, groped in the air, then settled on the back of Eleanor's head. He could feel her breath heating its way through his flannel pants, onto the private skin of his thighs. Beneath his hand her skull felt strangely large and round, solid as a cannonball. Then his hand moved from her head to her neck, which was surprisingly fragile, and as she snuggled her head in closer, his fingers reached down to caress her spine, and then finally, sliding along the soft surrounding flesh, down her spine to the warm plateau at its base, the place where he used to hold her when they used to make love.

The year he turned fifty-one Maurice decided that in two years time he would take a leave-of-absence from teaching. To make the waiting pass more quickly, he registered for a night course in Italian. Dressed in his blue serge suit, carrying a briefcase full of exam papers, he turned up for the first evening full of dread that he would be too old to do anything but make a fool of himself.

But after a few months he had zipped through the beginner's classes and could almost understand Italian movies on television. One night he went to a party given by one of the members of the class, a woman about his age — a widow who planned to spend her husband's estate "travelling through Europe like Henry James." She was taking classes, she revealed, not only in Italian, but also in French and Spanish. "Romance is my specialty," she confided to Maurice after the second glass of wine in her impressive penthouse apartment. "When are you going to Europe? It's a pity we can't travel together but what would people say?"

On his way out the door Maurice's legs tangled

with a cat streaking down the hall. "Stop it," a voice called out. Maurice, who'd had cats as a boy, reached down and picked the creature up. It came willingly into his arms and was purring contentedly on his shoulder when the owner of the voice, a young woman carrying a wicker basket, appeared.

"Just hang on for a moment. Would you mind carrying it? I'm afraid it won't go back in the basket." So he took it to the elevator and then down the elevator to the parking lot where the young woman, her name was Judith, had her car. He had to get in the car with her, so the cat wouldn't escape, and then she offered to drive him home if only he would carry the cat once more — please — from the car into her apartment. She explained that she had promised to keep the animal for a friend who was going — of all places — to Italy for a vacation, but that the cat, when she came to collect it, wouldn't let her pick it up.

"It's the most ridiculous thing. I mean, she only likes men it turns out. I don't know why he didn't get his brother to take it instead."

After Maurice brought the cat into her apartment, the ground floor of one of those downtown houses near the university, she offered him "a cup of coffee, or something," which turned out to be a glass of scotch. And then she said: "Well you've seduced the cat, what about me?" Maurice, awkward, began to blush, but before the blood could find its way to his cheeks she was kissing him, then she took his hand and pulled it under her sweater.

The parting was at least dramatic. To admit less would have been uncharitable. It happened one night in a hotel in Florence, a small *pensione* whose name Judith had gotten from a friend and carried with her in her book of addresses for, she claimed, at least five years. "Who would have ever guessed," she asked, as they came to the building's undeniably charming façade, "that I would be staying here one day? I mean, you can imagine the state I was in when I wrote down the address." Maurice, who knew he was supposed to be imagining a scene from the past with which Judith had presented him — a series of neurotic but artistic dashes across North American and Europe filled with hilarious adventures and innocent good fun — imagined instead the following: Judith sprawled naked on the bed of a young man whose poetic equipment hung primarily between his legs; Judith, her teeth stained purple by red wine, laughing in her wild way at some perfectly inconsequential joke; Judith rolling over like a cat to have her breasts stroked once more by the nameless poet before going off to her job in a health-food bakery; Judith taking out her address book so that she and the nameless wonder could exchange telephone numbers; Judith succumbing to a few last-minute caresses and being late for work; Judith finally writing down not only the name of her seducer but the name of the hotel where he claimed to have learned his amorous techniques.

Of course it had been raining; that spring it seemed that the sun came out only once a week, a brief obligatory flash at the end of a grey and inescapable chain of showers, downpours and drizzles, so that when they had stood at the desk to register Maurice felt uncomfortably wet, uncomfortably aware of the way his thinning white hair was plastered to his scalp. And when they went to their room to deposit their bags and get ready for dinner, Judith insisted on taking a shower to get

warm, so that while Maurice was sitting on the bed
changing out of the socks that had gotten soaked
through the holes in his desert boots, he was treated
to the sight of Judith standing under the hot spray,
Judith cupping and soaping herself like an irresistible young nymphet, finally Judith emerging naked and dripping, her nipples glowing like neon
lights from the heat of the shower and the friction
of the towel; and for the first time since their arrival
in Italy he wanted her, really wanted her, but even
as he stood to embrace her she turned away, an
instinctive refusal that she would have denied had
he accused her of it, and began dressing quickly,
slapping her rosy skin to keep warm.

The comedy of the shower, Maurice was able to
realize later when her leaving gave him time for
reflection, was the first act of a play which he
hadn't yet realized he was attending. It was only
later that he deduced Judith must have made her
plans several days before. This meant, for example,
that while he was changing his socks and promis-
ing to buy himself a new pair of shoes, she would
have been rehearsing her own part which included
the big farewell scene followed by a trip to the
airport and the taking of an already-reserved plane
to a destination where she knew she was awaited.

At the time, Maurice was left feeling only slightly
uneasy, slightly ashamed of himself for desiring
Judith when she was enjoying the healthy subcuta-
neous bounce of her own youthful skin rather than
thinking of the dirty old man to whom she had
pledged herself so faithfully, so irreversibly, that for
him to doubt her love and durability would have
been a total betrayal of her young heart.

The second act began at dinner as Judith raised

her head coyly to the waiter and asked for a bottle of something special but not too expensive. When the wine was poured, she raised her glass and toasted Maurice: "Thank you for Italy," she said. With that Maurice had experienced a little pinprick of anticipation, just enough to draw blood, just enough to wake him up and make him realize that something was happening. Between comments on the food, Judith reminisced about the various places they had seen. It was a thin portion of the script — like her poetry, Maurice thought later, her plays were dependent on blood and one liners. Nonetheless the essential was established: Italy was always discussed in the past; plans for their future were referred to only vaguely, like a dream already forgotten. While she chattered, Maurice watched Judith's face. It was a face he had found immensely attractive. Her black hair was in contrast to skin so white it was almost transparent. In certain lights, though not in the light of the restaurant, he could see fine blue veins lacing her temples. Her cheekbones were strong, her nose perfectly narrow and straight, her chin the shape of a heart. The only weakness was her eyes, which were a watery green, also transparent. Looking at her eyes, Maurice wondered if they were somehow the shallow lake of his dream, with sandy infertile depths that indicated good swimming but no future.

The third act was more vigorous. A good strong climax after the dawdling over coffee and dessert. "I've been thinking of going to England," Judith said. They were back in the room and Judith had poured herself a glass of the brandy she had bought at the Lester B. Pearson International Airport's duty-free. "England," Maurice said. "I think I'll

stay here." He couldn't believe his own calm voice.
Judith was sitting on the bed. He saw a small grin
break through the surface and then quickly disap-
pear. In the two years since they had started sleeping together, Maurice had always presumed he was
going to pay a terrible price for this ridiculous
flirtation with youth.

"We could meet in a month or so," Judith said.

"Are you leaving tonight?"

"In the morning."

"Do you need money?" The surface was broken
again, this time by a flush of embarrassment.
Maurice remembered the final scene with his wife, a
much uglier scene in which he had broken down
and cried while begging her to stay. At the time he
had felt a perverse pride in his ability to feel
emotion, his lack of ability to control himself.
Now, to his surprise, he felt no sense of bereave-
ment at all. It was a gift of the dream, he thought to
himself; the dream had prepared him.

"I have some traveller's cheques," Judith said.
"And I can stay at a friend's. A woman," she hastily
added.

"I think I'll take a bath," Maurice said.

"Don't you want to go for a walk? It's our last
night here."

"You go ahead."

Then he went into the bathroom and shut the
door. While he was running the water Maurice
looked at himself in the mirror. He could feel his
heart beating rapidly, a sense of tension. But it
wasn't painful. Then he sat in the steaming tub and
continued reading the mystery novel he had started
the night before. There were actually a few minutes
when he forgot that Judith was leaving. Then he

realized that if she hadn't been leaving he wouldn't have shut the door; nor would he have read his book, because as on other nights she would have come in and sat on the toilet while he bathed and discussed the sights they were going to see the next day. This made him feel old and heavy. It was a struggle to stand up and dry himself. He tried to remember if he had heard the door close. The night his wife had announced her departure she had gone right away, taken a taxi to the house of her new boyfriend. He had been left alone in the apartment to get drunk and feel sorry for himself. But now, when he had dressed, he opened the bathroom door to find Judith lying calmly naked in the bed. She was reading, too, the sheets and blanket pulled down so that her breasts peeked out like baby seals.

"Make love to me tonight," she said.

That was the fourth act: sex. It took a long time, Judith was more aroused than usual, and in her arousal she coaxed him along for a repeat performance. But Maurice felt his body was simply going through the routines; even while Judith sighed with pleasure, real or faked, he found himself sinking back into the calm sobriety of his dream, the warm tribal feeling of the friends he had never met. When it was over Judith told him again how much she loved him, how grateful she was for the trip to Italy. The trip, Maurice thought, had lasted only a month. What about the other two years they had shared together, or at least pretended to share? At the time they had seemed to him the highest reality he had ever experienced, an unexpected and passionate flowering after years of somnolence, a triumph of passion over age; but that was at the time.

When he opened his eyes in the morning and saw that she was gone, his first reaction was a sigh of relief. To keep young for her — he remembered she had once said of another man, one his own age, that he must wake up smelling like an overflowing ashtray — he had stopped smoking cigarettes. Now he quickly dressed and, without shaving, went downstairs and across the street to a café where he bought a package of cigarettes. Then he ordered a beer, followed by numerous cups of strong coffee which he drank while greedily smoking as he read the sports section of an English-language newspaper.

After he had paid his bill and was waiting for the receipt he caught sight of himself in the mirror: a red-faced man with white hair and a St. Francis fringe of beard who looked like an old-fashioned professor taking early retirement to spend his declining years touring Europe. With Judith, of course, he had been someone else — a potent older man still in the swim of sex and success — but as he counted his change — in front of Judith he had always been embarrassed — he decided to cross the street to the hotel and take a nap before lunch.

The fifth and final act of Judith's tragi-comedy began while Maurice was getting ready not for this nap but a similar one two days later. At the moment he discovered Judith had left him a note. It was in his shoe, and he had already walked on it for a dozen hours. It hit the floor with a slightly sweaty thump. He was still in Florence, still at the same hotel, still luxuriating in his new-found freedom.

Dear Maurice,

I wish I could be with you reading this note, but I guess that's like wanting to be at your own funeral. I love you very much, more than I have ever loved anyone else, and that frightens me. In one month exactly I will come back to Florence, and I will meet you at the restaurant where we had our "Last Supper." So if you want me, I'll be there. No questions, no answers, all I can offer you is myself.

Love

And after "love" she had written, of course, nothing at all, because it was their habit never to sign their love notes, ever since Judith had written her poem "Names Are Too Anonymous," which had won second prize in a national contest sponsored by the Canadian Broadcasting Corporation.

Hoping to end Act Five and bring the curtain down, Maurice disposed of the note. Carefully folding it up along its original creases, he held it briefly in the palm of his hand, then tossed it from the bed where he was sitting through the door of the bathroom and into the wastebasket under the sink. There was no applause. He reached for his red Michelin guide to Italy and began flipping through it. Since Judith's departure a strange and unidentifiable tune had been making its way to the surface: now finally he could hear it — "The Isle of Capri." One of the summers at the cottage, an early and unclouded summer, Eleanor had taught him to tango to "The Isle of Capri," and so every time the song came on the radio they would leap to their feet

and dance through the crowded rooms of their
cottage, out onto the screened porch and then,
when the black-fly season was over, down the pine-
shaded path to the beach where they would strip off
their clothes and plunge into the lake, humming
the chorus.

Maurice lit a cigarette. It was the first time since
his resumption of smoking after Judith's departure
that he had smoked a cigarette in the hotel room
that they had shared. He imagined Judith lying in
bed with her new lover in London, idlying flipping
on the television set for some light entertainment
between rounds. On his desk was the bottle of duty-
free scotch. Maurice stubbed out his first cigarette,
lit a second one, took a tentative swallow straight
from the bottle. Several times he had cut himself
while shaving along the edges of his beard, to say
nothing of the ragged patch on the left cheek that
resulted from a slip of the scissors while giving the
beard a post-shave trim. Also, last night, his glasses
had fallen to the floor while he was reading himself
to sleep and then he had stepped on them in the
dark when he got up to urinate, so that one of the
arms was bent. He felt too, though perhaps this was
only paranoia, that his skin had deteriorated very
quickly. He remembered something he'd read once
about essential hormones that were a by-product of
orgasms; somehow their sudden cessation had
made the skin of his neck extremely sensitive and he
had developed an uncomfortable rash. Ordinarily,
or at least formerly, he would have told Judith
about it and, as with his many other physical
complaints and hallucinations, she would have
comforted and cured. A pill, a bottle of lotion. But

now she was gone, so it was up to Maurice to go to the *farmacia*. At the crucial moment his Italian failed: while attempting to explain what he wanted he found himself absolutely silenced, waving his hands helplessly and pointing at his neck. Finally the good-natured clerk brought him a bottle which, when Maurice got back to his hotel room and translated the label with the aid of his dictionary, turned out to be very expensive baby shampoo.

He lifted the scotch to his lips again. In Winnipeg, when he was a boy, drunks would sometimes come to the door asking for money. His mother would always refuse them cash, but if there was food in the house she would make one of her "health" sandwiches, rye bread with cheese and jam. The prospect of a rye bread, cheese and jam sandwich was less than appealing. Maurice went to the bathroom and turned on the hot water. When he had cleansed himself with the Italian baby shampoo he packed his suitcases and left the hotel.

Once in his car he began to drive randomly, taking the streets that were easiest to turn onto, until he found a sign for Assisi. When he got there he parked near the centre of town, hauled out his guidebook, and went dutifully to worship at the recommended sights. In front of each painting, each work of sculpture, he first read the guide to find out what he was supposed to be looking at and then he would carefully appraise what was in front of him to make sure that no detail escaped him. He stayed in the hotel that he and Judith — in better days — had pre-selected together — and to cover his embarrassment at eating alone he read and re-read the guide at lunch and at supper. At the end of four

days he had seen absolutely everything — twice —
and had run out of the courage required for restaurant eating. Still consulting his book he drove to
Sienna. There he spent a week. But instead of
looking at paintings he found himself spending his
time walking aimlessly through the town. To make
the evenings pass more quickly he bought a bottle
of wine every afternoon. This he would drink in his
hotel room while writing home — at first postcards
to his friends in Toronto, then two long, sentimental letters to Eleanor which ran to a dozen pages
each. None of these were mailed, because when he
re-read them they seemed to be written in the voice
of a stranger. As he ripped the letters up and put
them into the wastebasket he considered returning
to Toronto — a thought which crossed his mind
every day, but then remembered, as he also did every
day, that he had rented out his apartment for the
year of his leave. The next morning he got into his
car and drove on the superhighway towards Milan.
His intention was to turn in the rented car at the
airport and fly to Paris, where he had a cousin who
worked at the British Embassy. While having lunch
at a roadside café he ran into an American couple
who heard his halting Italian and insisted he sit
with them. They were from California. He told
them he was an insurance salesman from Montana.
After a very alcoholic lunch the wife forced upon
him her copy of her favourite book, *Even Cowgirls
Get the Blues*, and Maurice, too drunk to keep
driving, spent the afternoon reading in his car.
Then he got off the superhighway and found
himself driving on a twisting road that led high
into the Tuscan hills. It began to rain; the rain was
joined by a thick mist. Exhausted by the hairpin
turns, he stopped at a hotel and rented a room. He

stayed there and read for three days. When he started driving again he found himself in high pine-covered mountains. There was still snow between the trees and he became so homesick for Canada that he stopped at the next small town and rented a room again. This hotel was owned by a man with a brother in Vancouver, so when he saw Maurice's passport he insisted Maurice eat with the family. After a long drunken dinner Maurice slept as though in a coma. The next day the owner filled him with coffee, then dragged him off to see the hunting preserve which it was his job to guard between seasons.

As they walked through the pine forests Maurice, breathing the clean mountain air, felt Judith slipping away. The owner had a rifle slung over his shoulder. When a rabbit bolted from under a hedge the rifle was suddenly up in the air; there was a sharp explosion and the rabbit lay bleeding its life out in the white snow. Back at the hotel Maurice split wood for the fire while dinner was being made. The Italian pine was fibrous and stuck to the blade of the axe, but even when it began to rain again Maurice kept working, feeling deep in his dream now, more contented than he had since his summers at the cottage.

It was a week before he left. At the car the owner of the hotel stepped forward to embrace him; for the first time in his life Maurice put his arms around another man. It was a strange sensation: a muscled bellied body pressing into his own. From that point on he drove without destination, making his way slowly to the coast and then ambling around until finally, as if by coincidence, he arrived in Florence on the appointed day.

He could never have found the hotel on purpose,

but trapped in a maze of one-way streets he arrived. When he checked in there was a two-week-old postcard from Judith, saying nothing about their meeting but mentioning only that she was in London and, again, thanking him for their time in Italy.

Nor was Judith at the restaurant that evening. But Maurice sat down, ordered a bottle of wine and began reading a British newspaper. By now he had a plan. After another day in Florence he would drive to Rome, spend a week walking the city, then fly back to Canada. He would arrive at the beginning of April. A perfect time to rent a cottage so that he could spend the rest of his leave living on water until he could start teaching again.

As he was thinking about this plan, a plan that had been formulating itself since the week in the mountains, he saw a family coming into the restaurant. It was unclear what drew his eye, something about the children — a girl of about ten who was very pretty and very restrained, and a brother who was somewhat younger but walked in a very strange and jerky fashion, as if he were drunk and about to fall over.

When he sat down the boy spread his arms wide, then clapped his hands to his chest while he leaned his head forward until it fell with a loud clink onto the empty soup-plate. Following the sound of bone against porcelain there was a low animal moan. The boy's mother, a plump, worried-looking woman, put her arm around him and began to murmur soothingly. The father was larger: a broad-shouldered man with a generous stomach and large ears, red with embarrassment, that protruded like

rigid wings from his head. While mother soothed
son, father showed daughter the menu. Her hands
were folded together and her eyes closed; as her
father talked she leaned over to listen, a polite little
princess, her eyes finally opening to look dutifully
at the difference choices.

He was sitting close to the family's table; without
looking directly at them he could see the waiter
approach, take their order. The father spoke
quickly, as if to tell the waiter that if the food came
right away there would be no further incidents.
Speed, at all costs, *speed*. In fact, Maurice told
himself as he started his second glass of wine, speed
— so far as the boy was concerned — was exactly
what was impossible because his lines of communi-
cation had been destroyed.

As if to confirm this the boy began gesticulating
wildly just as the waiter turned away. Then he
began to talk — or at least it might have been
talking, but really what was being emitted was a
new series of moans, varying wildly in tone and
pitch. This time both the father and the mother
leaned over him and spoke urgently. Then the
mother took one of the boy's hands and held it
firmly between her own.

Maurice's first course finally arrived. It was a
pasta dish, the specialty of the restaurant according
to the waiter, but it was covered in cheese burned
black at the edges. As Maurice was taking his first
bite the boy knocked his soup-plate from the table,
and when his father bent to retrieve it the boy leapt
to his feet and sprang towards Maurice.

His eyes were dark and burning, his face was
scarlet, his mouth was twisted into a black grimace.

As the boy's father tried to pull him back the boy opened his mouth wide and Maurice saw, as the boy began to scream, that he had no teeth.

Unable to stop himself, Maurice stood up to leave. The boy squirmed free and flew into Maurice's chest, wrapping his arms and legs around him and screaming into his coat.

Maurice was still shaking as he walked back to the hotel. Twice he almost stepped directly in front of cars, and both times, pulling himself back, he stumbled. He could feel the eyes of passers-by swinging to him, the way his own eyes had instinctively swung back to the boy in the restaurant. When he got to his room Judith was lying on the bed, reading. He saw his suitcase open by the dresser; the crumpled clothes had been taken out, neatly folded and replaced. Judith stood up and stepped towards him.

"I came to the restaurant but there was such a scene I thought it would be better to meet you here. Forgive me?"

She put her arms around him, gently, but as he closed his eyes his first reaction was to feel again as he had in the restaurant, a stunned inner silence as the boy clung to him, then the flurry of hands tearing at him and the boy as he had fallen to the floor, the boy still screaming until finally the father had the boy in his arms and was rushing him out the door. He remembered looking around the restaurant as he sat down again, finished his glass of wine and asked for a cup of coffee. He hadn't seen Judith then, she must have come earlier, but he had seen the way the girl, serene, had turned to her mother and asked if they were going to wait for their meal or leave right away.

Now it was Judith who was guiding him to the bed, where she made him lie down and took off his shoes. Eventually he put an arm around her and she rolled closer to him.

"I missed you." Her warm hand had searched its way inside his shirt, was caressing his chest as he shivered. Her eyes were closed and her face was calm and dutiful. Maurice looked up at the ceiling and then towards the door. He imagined Judith watching herself soothing him, watching herself as she extended her caresses, watching as she began to cover his neck with soft kisses, watching as her kisses moved from his neck to his chest to his belly.

"I had to learn something about myself," Judith whispered, or at least that was what he thought he heard as she undressed him. He began to shiver again so she pulled the covers over them and lay right on top of him, hugging him to make him warm. Maurice closed his eyes. The next thing he knew it was the middle of the night and he was making love to Judith.

"I knew we would never get divorced," Eleanor had said. That, too, in the middle of the night, after a reunion salted with its own passion. She had announced this while smoking a cigarette; Maurice, sipping at a glass of water and finding himself unable to stay in bed, instead paced about the apartment thinking how odd the familiar furniture looked in such a strange place.

The apartment had faced the expressway, so he was able to open the curtains and watch the streams of headlights travelling in and out of the heart of the city.

"I know it's crazy, we haven't even seen each other for two years, but I still love you. I admit I

made a mistake. I didn't mean to hurt you. It's just
that I had to find something out about myself.
What I found was that I was an old-fashioned girl,
just like the girl I always was. Let's get back
together, have children, live happily ever after."

Then she had gone to the kitchen to make coffee.
While the water was boiling and Eleanor was
talking about the house they would move into, the
cottage they would find to rent in the summer
again, the names they would give to their children,
Maurice had tried to imagine himself saying no.
The word wouldn't come out of his mouth so
instead he simply got dressed and walked out of the
apartment. On the way down in the elevator he had
broken into laughter, then laughed at himself
laughing.

Even driving across the city he couldn't believe he
had made such an escape. He was sure the gods
would strike him dead in a traffic accident, but
when he got back to his apartment he was still
alive. The first time the telephone rang he didn't
answer it. The second time he picked it up. Eleanor
told him that he was a bastard and that she never
wanted to see him again. Before he could protest
she hung up.

"I want us to be together forever," Judith said. "I
want to be with you. Will you let me?"

"Yes," Maurice said. He fell sleep thinking about
the lake of his dreams, the neighbours he had never
met.

Racial Memories

Racial Memories

The beard of my grandfather was trimmed in the shape of a spade. Black at first, later laced liberally with white, it was also a flag announcing to the world that here walked an orthodox Jew. Further uses: an instrument of torture and delight when pressed against the soft ticklish skin of young children, a never empty display window for the entire range of my grandmother's uncompromising cuisine. To complement his beard my grandfather — indoors and out — kept his head covered. His indoor hats were *yarmulkahs* that floated on his bare and powerful skull; the hats he wore outside had brims which kept the sun away and left the skin of his face a soft and strangely attractive waxy white. White, too, were his square-fingered hands, the moons of his nails, his squarish slightly-gapped teeth, the carefully washed and ironed shirts my grandmother supplied for his thrice-daily trips to the synagogue. A typical sartorial moment: on the day before his seventieth birthday I found him outside on a kitchen stepladder wearing slippers but no socks, his suit-pants held up by suspenders, his white shirt complete with what we used to call bicep-pinchers, his outdoors hat — decked out in style, in other words, even though he was sweating rivers while he trimmed the branches of his back-yard cherry trees.

Soon after I met him, I began remembering my grandfather. Especially when I lay in bed, the darkness of my room broken by the thin yellow strip of light that filtered through the bottom of my door. Staring at the unwavering strip I would try to make it dance. "Be lightning," I would say. "Strike me dead; prove that God exists." And then I would cower under my sheets, waiting for the inevitable. That was when I would remember my grandfather. Standing alone with him in the big synagogue in Winnipeg, the same synagogue where he must have sought God's guidance in dealing with Joseph Lucky, looking up at the vaulted ceilings, holding his hand as he led me up the carpeted aisle to the curtained ark where the Torah was kept.

And then he showed me the words themselves. God's words. Indecipherable squiggles inked onto dried skin not so different from the tough dry calluses on my grandfather's palms.

Also full of words was the high bulging forehead of my grandfather. Everything he said to me in English, which he spoke in a gently accented cadence I had difficulty understanding, he would repeat in Hebrew, which I couldn't understand at all. Cave-man talk, I would think, listening to the guttural sounds. He showed me, too, the separate section where the women sat. I was amazed at this concept of the women being put to one side, just as later I was to be amazed to discover that when women had "the curse" they spent their nights in their own dark beds, left alone to bleed out their shame.

My great-great Uncle Joseph, the one after whom I was named, served in the cavalry of the Russian czar. This is true, and I still have a photograph of a bearded man in full uniform sitting on a horse in the midst of a snowy woods. After two years, during which he was promoted once and demoted twice, my ancestor deserted and made his way across Europe to a boat which took him to Montreal. From there he caught a train on which, the story goes, he endeared himself to a wealthy Jewish woman who owned a large ranch in Alberta. We could pause briefly to imagine the scene: minor-key *War And Peace* played out against a background of railway red velvet, cigar smoke and a trunk filled with souvenirs. Unfortunately the lady was married, so my uncle ended up not in the castle but out on the range, riding wild mustangs. (Also, it has been claimed, singing Yiddish folk songs to the animals as they bedded down beneath their starry blankets.)

And then my Uncle Joseph struck it rich. Sitting around the campfire one night, he re-invented the still with the help of an old horse trough and a few lengths of hose. All this is according to my father; he was the historian-in-exile, but that is another story. The rest of the family claims he was only trying to make barley soup. Maybe that explains how my uncle became known as Joseph Lucky.

Having made his fortune and his name, Joseph Lucky began sending money to the relatives. We've all heard about those Russian Jews: semi-Cro-Magnon types covered in beards, furs, dense body hair, living without flush toilets or electricity in a post-feudal swamp of bone-breaking peasants, child-snatching witches and wicked landowners. Having helped his blood relations through the evolutionary gate of the twentieth century — to say nothing of destroying the racial purity of his adopted homeland — my uncle asked only one thing in return: that the newcomers settle in Winnipeg, well away from his field of operations. When they got established, he came to pay a visit. By this time the wealthy Jewess had died and, because of a jealous husband, my uncle Joseph had moved on from his life on the range to "business interests." Another photograph I possess: Joseph Lucky standing on the Winnipeg train platform, winter again, wearing matching fur coat and hat and framed by two enormous suitcases which my father tells me were made from "soft brown leather you could eat."

This was before the First World War, before my father was born. Also before the War was my uncle's demise. What had happened was that for causes unknown he was put in jail. After a few months he wrote to his nephew, my grandfather. The letter was written in Yiddish, using Hebrew characters — the same formula which my grandmother employed to torture my mother decades later. I've seen the letter; my grandfather showed it to me when I was a child. He opened the envelope and out blew the smell which made a permanent cloud in my grandparents' house, a permanent storm-cloud to be exact, always threatening to rain down the pale greenish soup that my grandmother claimed was all her frail stomach could support.

My grandfather was a strong man. Once, when a neighbour's shed was burning down, he carried out two smoke-damaged pigs. The image of my grandfather, wearing his inevitable satin waistcoat and box *yarmulkah*, walking down the street with a sow over each shoulder, has never seemed improbable to me. I can imagine him, too, poring over the letter from his benefactor. Caught between his duty to help a relative, his distaste for my uncle's way of life and his own poverty. According to my father, my grandfather never answered the letter. Instead, after waiting two weeks he gathered what cash he could and took a train for Edmonton. When he arrived he discovered Joseph Lucky had died of food poisoning and that his body had been claimed by someone whose name had not been recorded. My grandfather always feared that his delay had killed Joseph Lucky. That is why my father felt obliged to give me his name. Also because, he always insisted, Joseph Lucky had likely died not of food poisoning at all, but had been bribed away from the jail (body claimed by an "unrecorded stranger"! — who could believe that?) by a rich client and spent the rest of his days happily riding some faraway range.

"If you could credit a Jewish cowboy . . .," my mother would protest and shake her head. But that was where Joseph Lucky was lucky, I didn't have to be told. Somehow he had escaped being Jewish, wiggled out from under his fate and galloped off into that carefree other world where you were not under a life sentence or, to be more exact, perhaps you were under a life sentence of mortality (even an assimilated Jew finds it hard to believe in Heaven) but you had been promoted to a different part of the sentence: instead of being the object, you were the subject.

"Did you hear the one about the rabbi's wife?"

"No," I say. We are lying in the centre of the school football field, six of us in a circle, face to face with our bodies extended like the spokes of a wagon-wheel. It is late September, a cool heartbreaking twilight. At the word "rabbi" my stomach has suddenly tensed up and my hipbones start to press against the hard ground.

"This sausage salesman comes to the door . . . Are you sure you haven't heard it?" The five of us are the offensive backfield of our high-school football team: the wheel of which I am the only Jewish spoke.

"I'm sure," I say. I look up over at the boy who is talking. The fullback. A power runner known as Willy "Wild Bill" Higgins. He's the one we need when it's late afternoon, November, and gusts of cold rain are sweeping down the river valley and turning us into sodden little boys who want to go home. That's when Wild Bill — it's me who gave him the name — drives forward with his cleats spitting out gobs of mud, knees pumping up into the face of anyone crazy enough to tackle him.

"All right," he says, "forget it. Don't get your cock in a knot."

All evening, over my homework, I'm left wondering. Something to do with circumcision no doubt. Animal sex? Two weeks ago a girl I asked to a dance told me her father wouldn't let her go out with a Jew. I'm at my sixth school in ten years but I still can't get used to breaking the ice. Can't get used to the fact that it never breaks.

At eleven o'clock the phone rings. It's another spoke of the wheel — a small spoke, like me. "Don't let dickface get you down," he says. The first thing I think is how glad I am that this is happening over the telephone, so my friend can't see my eyes swelling up with unwanted tears.

Idiot, I say to myself. *Thin-skinned Jew* "Doesn't matter," I say aloud. "Except that maybe I missed a good joke."

Peter Riley laughs. He's a skinny Irish kid whose father has lung cancer. Sometimes, after school, I go home with him and we sit in the living-room with his father, feeding him tea and watching him die. "She says she only eats kosher," Peter Riley says.

I start a fake laugh, then stop.

"Not funny?"

"Not funny to me."

"Join the club," Peter Riley says.

"What club?"

"You name it."

"The Wild Bill Fan Club," I say, a little chunk of the past — another school, another group of boys — jumping unbidden out of my mouth.

Leonard lived above the garage attached to the house my grandfather bought after he moved to Toronto to be nearer the brothers, sisters, aunts, uncles, cousins, etc. The spider's web of relatives in Toronto didn't include my own parents: they had already learned their lesson and were hiding out in Ottawa, on their way to greener fields. As a gesture to family solidarity, however, they had sent me to the University of Toronto. There I was not only to carry my parents' proud banner in the world of higher learning, but to act as unofficial delegate and/

or sacrifice. Leonard, not a relative but a paying boarder, was also at the university; ten years older than I, he had the exalted status of a graduate student in religious philosophy. "He doesn't eat kosher," my grandmother confided to me in the kitchen, "you can tell by his smell, but he goes to *shul* every morning and he doesn't make noise."

In a room with my grandparents, Leonard was so well-behaved and courteous that he hardly seemed to exist. Once out of sight, however, he became the main subject of my grandmother's conversation. "Did you see how he wiped his mouth?" she always began, as though she had spent the whole time doing nothing but watching Leonard compulsively snatch at the napkin. And then Laura, a cousin slightly older than I who had sealed her reputation by going to a drive-in at age fourteen with a married man (self-made, rich from vending-machine concessions), would point out that once again the insides of Leonard's nostrils were flaming red because — she had seen him at it through his window — every night he spent an hour yanking out his nasal hairs in order to combat his other urges.

"Wanna see my place?" Leonard invited, while we were drinking tea after a sabbath lunch.

I followed him out the back door, along a path worn through the grass, and we arrived at the metal stairway leading up the outside of the garage to Leonard's room. Immediately I found myself thinking this arrangement was ideal because it allowed Leonard to come and go as he pleased, even bringing company with him if he wanted. Or could. An unlikely possibility I thought, following the shiny seat of Leonard's grey-and-black checked trousers up the final steps.

The first thing I noticed was the mirror where Leonard was reported to carry on with his nose. It hung above a dresser from which the drawers jutted out, each one overflowing. The cartoon chaos of the room continued. Piled over every available surface were dirty clothes, newspapers and magazines, empty pop bottles, wrappings from candystore food. Even the desk of the graduate philosopher was a tower of babble — unsteady stacks of library books interspersed with sheaves of folded paper. Ostentatiously draped over the back of the chair was a strangely mottled towel. Stepping closer I saw that the towel was, in fact, heavily stained with blood.

"War wounds," Leonard said.

At lunch I had already noticed Leonard's soft white fingers, his unmuscled arms blotched with freckles and covered with a sparse layer of white-orange fur.

"They're crazy for it then. Ever notice?"

I shook my head.

"Read Freud. The power of taboo. Close your eyes. Imagine it. You're in the dark with the woman of your dreams. The smell of sweat and blood. Smells so strong you can taste it. Get up from the bed and your dick is dripping with it."

My eyes weren't closed. I was looking at Leonard. His eyes were boring straight into my face. "You some kind of a pervert?"

Leonard looked puzzled. Encouraged, I continued with a further inspiration: "If you didn't pick your nose, it wouldn't bleed."

Leonard shook his head. "You're going to study philosophy, kid, you need to have an open mind. I told you the truth."

"Don't make me laugh. No woman in her right mind would come into this rat's nest for more than five minutes."

At which point Laura opened the door, came and stood by Leonard's chair, practically sticking her chest in his face while he patted her bum. "Isn't this great? Look, we're going to drive you downtown and then we'll pick you up later for dinner. Isn't this place unbelievable?"

Laura and Leonard are halfway up the greys, exactly at centre ice. From where I line up on defence I can see the steam billowing from their styrofoam cups of coffee. They grin at me. "Go get 'em," Leonard shouts and his voice echoes in the empty arena. This is intra-mural hockey, a house-league game taking place close to midnight. The only other spectators are a few couples who have discovered that the shadowed corners of the varsity rink are good for more than watching hockey.

My legs are tired. There are lines of pain where the blades of the skates, which don't quite fit me, press into the bones of my feet. One of my shoulders has already begun to ache as the result of a collision against the boards. Peter Riley looks back at me. He is our centre. A quick skater with dozens of moves and a hard wrist-shot, he is the only one who really knows how to play. The rest of us make up a supporting cast, trying to feed him the puck and to protect our goalie, a non-skating conscript whose main virtue is that he has the courage to buckle on his armour, slide across the ice in his galoshes and risk his life.

Most games we just give the puck to Peter and he scores with tricky unstoppable shots. Now we're in the finals and they've got the strategy to beat us. Two, sometimes three, players shadow Peter, sandwiching him every time he tries to dart forward. The rest of us are often left in the open but compared to these other bigger, stronger players, we are ineffectual midgets. Somehow, however, our goalie has risen to the occasion. With a couple of minutes to go in the game we are only one goal behind.

The referee looks back at us. I bend over my stick. My rear end is sore from numerous forced landings. Riley winks at me and then nods his head for good measure. I know what this signal — our only signal — is supposed to mean: when the puck is dropped he will gain control — then I am to skate by at full speed so that he can feed it to me and send me in.

As the puck bounces on the ice I'm already driving forward, and by the time I've crossed centre ice the puck — via Riley — has arrived at my stick. I'm alone, the crowd of two is screaming. I'm going as fast as I can but I can hear the ice being chewed up behind me, long powerful strides gaining on my short choppy ones. The hollow ominous sound of steel carving ice, Laura's amazingly loud voice — I lift my stick back preparing to blast the puck before I'm overtaken — and then something has hooked my ankles and I'm sliding belly-down.

No whistle so I'm up again. Peter has somehow recovered the puck from the corner and is waiting for me to get in front of the net. This time I'm going to shoot on contact, no waiting: again my stick goes back. Then I'm swinging it forward, towards the puck, already feeling the sweet perfect impact of the hard rubber on the centre of my blade,

already seeing the net billow with the tying goal.
Suddenly the curtain comes down. A blast to my
forehead so intense that I lose consciousness falling
to the ice. Get up, dazed, glove held to my head.
Start skating again, vision foggy, towards the puck,
until I see that everyone else has stopped, that my
glove and hockey stick are covered with red, that the
clouding of my vision isn't dizziness but a veil of
blood over my eye. Leonard and Laura are rushing
towards me.

There are words, too. "Jew. Eat it, Jew," I
thought I heard someone say. The words are rattling in my head like pebbles in a gourd but I'm too
confused to know who put them there. Laura's got
a handkerchief out of her purse, it's soaked in
perfume, soft white cloth with a pink stitched
border. The pebbles are still rattling in my skull
and I can't stand them, have to do something about
them, twist away from Laura and skate towards the
big boy with blood on his hockey stick.

But Peter Riley is already there. When the boy
hears me coming, turns towards me, Riley twists —
twists and straightens his legs as he sends an upper-
cut deep into the unpadded belly. Mine enemy
collapses to the ice retching. His team prepares to
rush ours. By now I have felt my cut with my bare
finger: a small gash above the left eyebrow that
opens and closes every time I move the muscles in
my face.

Before anything can happen there is a sharp blast
of the whistle. The referee, who is also the Dean of
Men and who hands out suspensions for fighting
— from the university, not just from hockey — is
holding the puck and standing bent over the spot
where he wants play to begin again.

"Sir," Riley says, "one of our players is bleeding."

"Have his friends take him to the hospital."

As I'm clumping along the wooden gangway, Laura's scented hanky pressed to my wound, Leonard is calling my dean a "Jew-baiting bastard, an anti-Semitic son-of-a-bitch who would have spent his afternoons cracking open teeth to get at their gold fillings."

By three o'clock in the morning, when I am sharing a mickey of rye with Peter Riley, my wound has been reduced to a small throbbing slice covered by a neat white patch. And Riley is telling me that the dean shook his hand as he left the dressing-room.

As I fall asleep, the words are still with me. I am lying in the dark. The first time I heard such words, such words said by other than my own, I was ten years old. I was in a new school that year, but friends had come quickly and life seemed suddenly to have grown wide and easy. Then one day, late in the fall, my friends turned on me. There were three of them. "Jew," one of them said. "Jew," said the other two. We had been standing in a vacant lot on the way home from school. Talking about nothing. One of them pushed me. A nothing push, not really a punch, something I wasn't sure whether or not to ignore.

"Jews are Christ-killers," one of them said.

"Christ-killers," the others repeated. The words unfamiliar to all of us.

Now I can see they didn't know what to do. Something their parents had said would have put them up to this, probably without intending anything specific.

There were more shoves. I shoved back. "Christ-killer," they were saying, still trying to convince themselves. "Run," one of them said.

"No."

"Run." said the biggest one. He slapped me across the face, knocking my glasses to the grass. When I bent to pick them up, he covered them with his foot. I reached anyway. As I pulled them out from his shoe he stamped on my hand.

"Run."

I held my glasses tightly. The other two boys, the ones I had thought were my friends, had backed away. Without my glasses their faces were foggy and distorted. I put my glasses on. My friends had pebbles in their hands.

"Run."

I ran, hating myself from the first step. As I did a shower of rocks fell gently on my back. One boy, the biggest, chased me. I was smaller but faster. I vaulted over the fence — clearing it the way I'd had to in order to become a member of the club they had invented — the Wild Bill Fan Club — then ran to the back door as the one boy still chased after me. As I opened the door, he reached in. To grab? To punch? A reflex action? I slammed the door on his hand.

For a week I walked back and forth from school alone. Stomach broiling. At night I couldn't wait to be in bed, alone, lights out. Then finally the world of fear I'd been containing all day in my belly could expand, spread out, swallow the make-believe theatre of pretend-niceness that surrounded me during the day. In the dark, instead of daring God to show himself as I used to, I listened for the sound of convoy trucks on the road, knocks at the door, policemen's boots on the stairs. And if they weren't going to come? I eventually had to ask myself. Did that mean that in this new world there was safety after all? That my great-great Uncle Joseph Lucky truly had led us out of the wilderness and into the promised land?

One afternoon recess, during the compulsory all-school no-rules soccer game, mine enemy was delivered. Head down, dribbling the ball forward at full speed, running straight at me while being chased by fifty screaming boys. An hour later we were standing on either side of the door of the principal's office. Him with scratched cheeks from the gravel he fell into when I tripped him, plus a swollen lip from the only punch I had managed to land; me with bloody nose and ribs re-arranged from the fight-ending bearhug.

I still remember the principal's suit. A blue-grey plaid too long for his short legs, worn cuffs, lapels sporting a maple leaf pin. In his hands, very small, was a thick leather strap. Without comment he reddened our palms. Then we were out in the hall again, the door closed behind us. No handshakes, no words of mutual consolation, no smiles. But by the time the school day had finished, the under-ground telegraph had turned us into folk heroes, victims and survivors of the principal's best, warmly united members of the Wild Bill Fan Club once more.

I am in Laura's bedroom. Laura is in her dressing

gown, then takes it off to try on her dress. Laura encased in sterile white brassiere and panties surrounded by tanned skin. The body is untouched, an uninhabited countryside, a national park waiting for its first visitor; but her face is the city. A long curved jaw stubbornly set. Lips painted what Peter Riley called "North Toronto Red." Brown eyes, Jewish eyes, eyes which I knew my friend found sympathetic and embracing, but which to me looked hardened with all the calculations they had made.

I am in Laura's bedroom because I have been delegated the task no one wants. Why me? Instead of, for example, my father? The explanation for this lies in other stories, stories too long and intertwined to tell, stories not about Joseph Lucky and Laura and Leonard, but stories about my parents. Most of all my father who had decided by now to complete his escape and was residing (with my mother, of course — herself a subject not to be broached without lengthy explanations) in Sydney, Australia where he was attempting to unknot the city's bus schedules.

"This is crazy. I'm supposed to talk you out of marrying my best friend."

"So talk me out."

"He's a shit. His father's dead and his mother drinks too much. So does he. His brother is a lawyer and makes deals with politicians. His sister goes to church on Sundays. Five years from now he'll be screwing his secretary. How's that?"

"You can do better."

"He's a Catholic. Secretly he hates Jews but he hasn't got the guts to say it. He's marrying you in order to destroy you. When you have children he'll drag them down the basement to a priest he has hidden in the furnace and baptize them.''

"At least we'll have a house.''

"Tell me,'' I suddenly say. As if I'm thinking about it for the first time, and maybe I am. "Why *are* you marrying outside? Really why?''

Laura looks at me. For a second it seems that my question has truly surprised her, cracked the shell. Then I realize that she's only waiting for me to back down. "I love him,'' she says. Her voice is so wooden as she pronounces this formula that I can't help believing her.

"But answer my question.''

"Crazy boy.''

She crosses the room to where I am sitting on her bed. Bends over me and kisses the scar above my eyebrow. Then my lips. A slow kiss that leaves me bathed in her taste and scent. "I couldn't marry a Jew. It would be like incest, if you know what I mean. Did I ever show you this? Grandpa gave it to me.''

Dear Nephew,
You will remember me. I am your wicked uncle, Joseph Lucky. A few years ago I came to visit you and the rest of those whom you call your family. As always, I brought gifts. As always, they were greedily snatched and then scorned. His money is dirty, they would like to say, since they have none. You alone wrote to thank me. I kept your letter, nephew, because I, a childless old man, wanted to dream about what might be possible. I imagined such things, nephew, as bringing you to live with me and making you a partner in my various

enterprises. That is the letter I should have written you because you might have been the one to change my fate. Too late now. Now I am in jail, starving because despite everything you might have heard about me I refuse to eat anything but kosher food. To tell the truth, even the smell of pork chops is enough to turn this old stomach. Nephew, I beg you to come and see that I am released, or at least fed. When you arrive I will give you the name of a lawyer who can arrange things.

Love from your fond Uncle—

"What about the other letter? The one my father has?"

"There were lots of letters. Each one written as though the others had somehow failed to arrive. Not all of them were sent to Grandpa either."

"And when he went to Edmonton?"

"He never went. No one did. They let him die because they were ashamed of him." Laura puts on her dressing gown and lights a cigarette. "You think Peter's cousins are on their knees right now? Begging Peter not to marry me?"

"They should be."

An hour later I am at Leonard's. Stiffening the spine so that I can report the failure of my mission to my grandparents. "You are the outsider," Leonard is explaining to me, "the perennial third man. You think it's because of your shiny metal mind. Forget it. You're outside because you're a Jew. And that's why Laura is marrying your friend. She grew up being outside and now she wants to be sure she'll be outside forever. Except that she won't because ten years from now the whole world will be people like you and Laura, people trying to get away from themselves. And you know what will happen then? Laura will decide she's unhappy. She'll start to drink or have an affair or run away to a kibbutz in Israel. The next time you see her, middle-aged, she'll say that she wasted ten years of her life. She'll ask you why you let her get married."

"Why did I?"

"Because you want to do the same thing."

Leonard was dressed in his *shul*-going suit. Black without stripes or flecks. Shiny seat bottom. Pockets padded with *yarmulkahs* and hankies just in case someone needed an extra. Soon we would be going to the bride's house, which was where the wedding would take place — under the supervision of a Unitarian minister who didn't seem to believe anything overly offensive.

"And you? I thought you were the one who was so hot for her."

After my grandfather's first heart attack Leonard had evolved from paying boarder to man of the house. Now he even had a job — as a history teacher at the Orthodox Synagogue Hebrew Day School. Leonard the responsible citizen was heavier, jowled and his hair was turning a dull grey at the temples. And then he smiled. With the memory of whatever had transpired between him and Laura, I thought at first, though what could have linked this prematurely middle-aged perpetual bachelor to the ripe and bursting Laura was hard to imagine. "Never," Leonard said. "I promised myself years ago to a young woman of strong character who takes care of her mother in Vancouver."

"And when did you meet her?"

"The summer I went to study in New York. She was on the Holocaust committee."

"How romantic."

Leonard gave me a look I hadn't seen since the day he explained his bloody shirt. "You're a fool. Helen is the perfect woman for me in every way." He turned to his desk. In his student days it had been heaped with scholarly texts. But since the summer in New York, the philosophical treatises had been pushed aside first to make room for bulky volumes on the Holocaust and then, more recently, for the history primers he needed for his job. From a drawer stuffed with letters he pulled a picture of a squarish-looking woman with a young smile and a surprising splash of freckles across her nose. "When her mother dies —"

My grandparents are waiting for me in their parlour. Like Leonard, like my grandfather, like Laura's own father waiting resignedly at home, I am dressed in a suit. An almost new suit, in fact, the one I bought a few months ago when I graduated from law school. Eventually I will wear the same suit, the same white shirt, the same gold cuff-links to my grandfather's funeral. The cuff-links were his gift to me on my Bar Mitzvah. On that occasion, a few weeks after my thirteenth birthday, I had needed new thick-heeled shoes to push me over the five-foot mark. One sideburn had started to grow, but not the other, and this unequal hormonal outburst had been accompanied by the very unmasculine swelling of one of my nipples. For some reason this swollen nipple ached when I sang, especially when my voice cracked in public, which it did dozens of times during the painful delivery of my *moftar*. Afterwards my grandfather, his breath thick with rye, had delivered me a bristly kiss and pinched my arm so lovingly that I carried the bruise for a month.

Now they are sitting stiffly and waiting, elderly patients bracing themselves for the bad news. Stubborn but helpless. I beg them to at least come to the reception, for Laura's sake. This is the compromise everyone has been hoping for — avoiding the wedding but joining the celebration.

My grandfather is looking placidly about the room. His most recent attack seems to have taken away his electricity. He is perpetually serene, almost vacant. Even his shining and muscular skull seems to have lost its power; now the skin is greyer, listless. I try to imagine what might be going on inside. Weather?

My grandmother is twisting her hands. Everything considered, she has big diamonds. "We'll go," she announces. "The mother of those bastard children was born a Jew and so the children can still be rescued, God willing, after the father has left."

"Assimilated," Leonard says. He pronounces the word slowly, savouring, then repeats it. First he stares at me — a Leonard who has emerged in the ten years since his own marriage, a Daddy Leonard with a rounded bulldog face, muscular cheeks, blue eyes that have spent so many long nights poring over his Holocaust documents that they have turned the skin surrounding them into dark craterholes — then he swings his head to Laura for confirmation. She nods. Laura whom I've known forever. Laura who is prettier than ever, but whose face seems more angular because she decided to replace her contact lenses with glasses when she started taking Hebrew lessons again.

I am sitting by the window. It's still open, a souvenir from the golden warmth of the October afternoon. Now it's evening and a cold breeze sucks at the back of my neck, but no one is thinking about the heartbreak of Indian summer.

Laura is kneeling on the floor. Her floor, the floor of the living-room of her and Peter Riley's North Toronto house. While she kneels she staples posters to sticks. NAZI JEW KILLER the posters all read.

"I can't believe how *assimilated* you are," Leonard says, pleased with himself now that he has found the word for me. "How *typical*. I won't say you're a coward. When it comes to being punched in the face, you're ready. When they call for volunteers to get baked, you'll probably run to the train. *Bravo*. But ask you to stick your neck out and stand up for yourself — all of a sudden you turn into a lawyer for some Jew-baiting creep."

"Listen to yourself," I say. "You're filled with hate. Do you think Jews are the only people in the world who have ever been killed? Even during the Second World War there were three million Poles who died. Gypsies were sent to concentration camps too. Do you think the Holocaust gave the Jews some sort of moral credit card? Do we get to trade our dead for Palestinians? Is it one for one or do Chosen People get a special rate of exchange?"

"I have never killed anyone. But I am proud of my people when they defend themselves."

"Violence poisons," I say.

"God is violent," Leonard comes back.

Bang-clack, bang-clack, goes Laura's stapler. Now she's finished her signs, a dozen of them. In a few minutes it will be time to carry them out to the family-size station-wagon. While the "family" — twin four-year-old daughters — sleeps, Peter is to babysit. And while Peter babysits, Laura and Leonard are to drive the signs out to the airport, where Leonard has been tipped off that an East German cabinet minister someone claims was once a concentration camp guard is to arrive for inter-governmental trade discussions.

Laura and Leonard stand up.

"I'll go with you," I say.

Leonard's face breaks open. "I knew you would." He moves forward, hugs me. All those years living above my grandparents and now he smells like they used to — the same food, the same soap, the same sickly sweet lemon furniture polish. I can't help smiling, thinking about Leonard's youth as I knew it: tortured nasal passages, a white towel soaked with what he claimed was menstrual blood.

We stand around for a moment while Leonard phones home. At the other end, apparently saying little, is his woman of perfect character, the devoted Helen who has borne him four children and seems to make a virtue of obeying Leonard. They live in the main house now — my grandparents left it to them — and the room above the garage is consecrated to books and pamphlets detailing the attempted destruction of the Jews. Lately they've added slides, films, one of those roll-up white screens with little sprinkles on the surface. You know what I mean.

We all drag the posters out the front door to the waiting station-wagon. A few leaves crackle and

drift in the cool breeze. Lights are on in all the
houses around us. It's the moment when children
have gone to bed, tables have been cleared, tele-
visions have been turned on or attaché cases opened.
We're on the lawn waiting for Peter to open the
back hatch when a neighbour walking his dog
stops to talk. The subject of conversation is, of
course, the weather, the growing possibility of
snow, the desire to spend one last weekend at the
cottage. Only while the neighbour is agonizing
over his big decision — whether or not to dig
trenches so that he can keep the cottage water
turned on until Christmas — does he notice the
NAZI JEW KILLER signs. He says he is going to dig
the trenches after all, if the weather is good, you
have to think of the future, and besides he has
always wanted his children to share his own dream,
a white Christmas in the country.

At the airport a small band of the faithful were
waiting on the fifth floor of the parking garage. We
got out of the car, distributed the signs. According
to Leonard's information, the former concentra-
tion-camp guard was due on an Air Canada flight
from London. The plan was to meet him at the
Passenger Arrivals gate.

  There were ten of us. Too many, with our NAZI
JEW KILLER signs, to fit into a single elevator.
Laura went with the first group — Leonard too —
so I was left with four strangers to descend in the
second shift. One of those strangers became you,
but only later. Sharing our elevator were two
passengers with their suitcases. At first they paid us
no attention — then, reading our signs, they shrank
back.

By the time we had left the elevator and were walking towards the Arrivals gate, Leonard's group was surrounded by airport security officials and police. We raised our own signs and began to approach them. But before we could be noticed Leonard had gotten into a shouting match with one of the officials. "Never lose your temper needlessly," Leonard had lectured us in the Riley living-room. But, as Laura told me later, Leonard had already called his friends at the television station and promised a confrontation. When photographers with television cameras on their shoulders and assistants carrying portable lights began to run towards the struggling group, Leonard turned towards them. Soon, the official forgotten, he had positioned himself in front of one of the cameras to make a speech about a country that denied its own citizens free expression while protecting foreign "criminals against humanity." Then there was one of those incidents that is not supposed to happen, a relic from other countries, other eras: just as Leonard was working himself to a climax, a policeman smashed his truncheon into the back of his head, sending him falling face forward onto the floor.

Later that night I could watch myself on the television news as I entered the circle of light, knelt above Leonard and turned him over so I could see on his face, running with blood, a half-smile of triumph. You weren't in the picture. "Communist," shouted a voice from off-camera, but no one laughed.

Driving to the liquor store Peter Riley and I are already drunk. Actually, we have been drinking all afternoon. It's the kind of day that deserves drinking, a Toronto December special that is cold but snowless, a gritty colourless day that merges pavement and sky. Peter's shirt is open. The tuft of red hair at the base of his neck has gone to flat silver; silver too is the colour of the red mop that used to peek out the holes and edges of his football helmet. To heighten the effect he's wearing a leather jacket left over from our university days; U of T 66 is blazoned across the back in white. Looking at him, at myself slumped uncomfortably beneath the seat belt, I am reminded of the men Peter Riley and I used to go and watch during the summer in Ottawa, fat and powerful men with big paunches and thick arms who played evening softball at the high school diamond. Strong but graceless, able to swat the ball a mile, but stumbling around the bases in slow motion, the evening athletes had always seemed an awesome joke to us. "Battles of the dinosaurs," we called their games, delighting in their strength, the kaleidoscope of grunts and sweat and beer-fed curses.

At the liquor-store parking lot we climb out of the car and stand, side by side, looking up at the clouds. We aren't two baseball players, I am thinking, among other things; we are two middle-aged lawyers, partners in a small firm. We are tense, over-tired, mind-fatigued businessmen taking a day off to drink ourselves into oblivion because it's the only cure we know for the fact that while eating lunch we reminded each other that Leonard had died exactly six weeks before. Not that either of us had ever considered ourselves admirers of Leonard. Still.

"Among other things" includes the sound of the dirt falling onto Leonard's coffin, his family's uncontrolled grief, the talk at the funeral about another martyr to anti-Semitism. You were present, silent, beautiful, though your face was pinched with cold. We started walking towards each other at the same time and before we had even told each other our names, I was asking you for your telephone number. Also at the funeral were the wide circle I see once every few years at such events. Aunts, uncles, cousins at various removes who have come not because they think of Leonard as a martyr or support his politics but because they remember Leonard as the faithful boarder who helped my grandparents through their old age, the daily *shul*-goer who, even when my grandfather was eighty years old, patiently shepherded him back and forth to the synagogue.

Some of the aunts, the uncles, the cousins at various removes are themselves getting old now. Short stocky men and women in their seventies, eighties, even the odd shrunken survivor who was born in the last century. Many of them, not all, were born in Russia and came out of the mythic peasant crucible to Canada where they gradually adorned themselves in suits, jewellery, houses, coats, stock-market investments until finally, at this group funeral portrait, they could be seen literally staggering under the weight of their success.

I find myself looking at Peter Riley's open shirt again. "For Christ's sake, do up the buttons, you'll get arrested."

"Undo yours," Peter Riley says. "In the name of the Wild Bill Fan Club, I formally dare you to undo your buttons."

"For Christ's sake," I say again, this time wondering why on this occasion it is Christ I invoke — Leonard must have been right. An occasion, to be

precise, on which Peter Riley and I have already
emptied one bottle of scotch, to say nothing of a few
beer chasers, and now find ourselves at 4:33 P.M. in
front of the Yonge Street liquor store in search of a
refill. Near the liquor store is a shop where we can
buy newspapers, mix, cigarettes, ice, candies. Even
twenty years ago, when we were under-age, we went
there to buy Coke for our rum.

"I'll go to the liquor store," I say, "you get the
other."

The scotch hits me while I am alone in the
heated display room. "The last of the big drinkers I
am not" is the sentence that comes into my mind —
spoken by my father. But my father is dead, possibly along with whatever part of me is his son.
"Never shit on your own doorstep," my father also
told me. Translation: you can go to bed with non-
Jewish girls, but don't bring them home. I move
down the counter and settle on a bottle of *The
Famous Grouse* scotch whisky. When I present my
order the cashier makes a point of staring at my
unbuttoned shirt. He has straight oiled hair into
which each plastic tine of the comb has dug its
permanent trench. My age or older. Skin boiled red
by repeated infusions of the product he is selling.
Looks a bit like Wild Bill near the end, I finally
decide, but not enough for me to tell him about the
fan club. I look into his eyes. Tough guy. He
doesn't flinch. Meanwhile the store is empty, we
could go on staring like this forever. "I'm having
an identity crisis," I imagine saying to him, "I
mean I was born Jewish but I don't feel comfortable
carrying NAZI JEW KILLER signs."

That night I dream about the hearse, a sleek

powerful limousine. You aren't in the dream but the rest of us are. We're sitting behind the driver: Laura in the centre, Peter Riley and I surrounding. Behind us is the coffin and its presence somehow makes us even smaller than we are, reminding us that Death is the queen bee and we humans are just worker bees keeping Death supplied. It is night-time, the time of night when time does not exist.

The hearse is carrying us down University Avenue. Wide, empty, stately, the street conducts us to the American Embassy where there is one other car, an ambulance with its rotating light winking "He's nuts" into the sky. The attendants, bored, are leaning against the ambulance and talking to the lone policeman.

Crouched on all fours, his weight on his knees and hands, Leonard is howling like a dog at the closed door of the American Embassy.

When he sees us he interrupts to wink, then turns back to his howling. After listening for a while I realize that his howl is in fact controlled, a merely moderate howl you can howl until dawn or at least until newspaper reporters arrive. I turn to relay this news to Laura and Peter Riley, but as I turn I see they have been transformed into the ambulance attendants, while I have somehow ended up on my knees, baying at the door. When Leonard tries to arrest me I leap at his throat, bringing him to the ground and tearing at him until I wake myself up with my screams.

At the funeral the men took turns throwing shovel-fuls of earth on the coffin. Into the silence small stones and earth rattled against the dull wood. I couldn't help listening, I couldn't help watching, I couldn't help crying at the thought of Leonard dead. At some point I discovered you were still standing beside me. Anonymous in your black coat, bare fingers gripping each other in the frozen air, thin black shoes with the toes pressed together. When the service was over we walked towards the parking lot, climbed into my car, drove to a hotel.

Now this hotel is my train. You are my benefactress, wealthy in the dark cream skin that you inhabit, the mysterious odours of your mysterious places, your eyes that becalm everything they see. Under your protection we ride our wild animals into the twilight. Until beneath our starry blankets we find a way to sleep — out on the range, in this room which hovers in an otherwise unmarked universe, which exists for no other purpose than the mutual exploration of mutual desire. *Assimilated*, as Leonard used to say; against our non-existent will we have been assimilated into this compromised situation — two unrecorded strangers claiming each other with words sight touch smell until we raise spark enough to join our foreign bodies.

Other Titles In This Series

Other Titles In This Series

Other Titles In This Series

Other Titles In This Series

924198

72499